People of the ER

People of the ER

Philip Allen Green MD

ISBN: 154822295X
ISBN 13: 9781548222956

For my family

Questions or Comments:

philipallengreen@hotmail.com

Contents

The People of the ER

Let me tell you about the other people of the emergency department, the people who live in the space between the notes.

The people of the ER.

They are the addicts at the end of addiction. They are the lost who have run out of things to lose. They are the drunks, the druggies, the haters, the handcuffed, and the ultimate have-nots.

In any given instant, in any given ER, if you just look hard enough, you can find them. They are scattered throughout the rooms, half hidden in the noise and chaos, tucked away here and there between the chest pains and traumas. It is easy to miss them, to walk right past them or even right through them. But not today.

Let's start with room one.

It has a man in it. His name is Steven. He is an alcoholic. Not the "Hi, my name is Steven, and I'm an alcoholic" kind of alcoholic—no, Steven is the ER kind of alcoholic. You've probably caught a glimpse of him before. At the very least you've seen your town's version, your town's Steven.

He is one of the ones who've been wadded up and tossed away by the world—a forgotten scrap of humanity, a scavenger who scurries away into the darkness when you flip on the security lights at 3:00 a.m. You can find him—you can find *them*—curled up on park benches and sprawled spread-eagled across the littered grass of nearly every downtown median. They are not the ones with the clever, handwritten signs asking for money. The true Stevens are too drunk to care. As you drive by, you tell your kids, "Those people are just sleeping," but you know the truth. They are beyond blackout drunk at 7:43 a.m.

The Stevens are everywhere.

In some ways, the Stevens are the true citizens of the world. Politics and borders are meaningless to them. They live and have lived in every country and every time since the dawn of history. They are their own tribe and their own people, the true nomads who wander and drift with the wind. In the winter they migrate south. When summer comes, they stumble their way back, bottle by bottle, to small towns and big cities the world over.

If you need to talk to Steven, or maybe just want to bring him a sandwich, follow the broken glass. It is a trail of a thousand shards shining in the sun. A trail of tragedy. Get down close on your hands and knees and take a deep breath. You will smell last night's booze. Your eyes will water, and your nose will burn as if you have just snorted a long line of industrial bleach.

Move your head ever so slightly, and the trail glistens. It lights up like a path of diamond dust. The clear glass of broken vodka bottles catches the rising sun just so. Lean even closer, and you will find beautiful reds, blues, and greens. They are the colors of smashed-up Mad Dog 20/20. Bottles dropped and broken, still dripping with fortified wine. They speckle the trail like paint whipped from a brush. Throw in a few gold flecks spilled from the shoplifted fifth of Goldschläger, and suddenly your trail of tragedy looks so damn beautiful that even you can't resist it. You have to follow it, to find its artist, to find its source.

So off you go, strolling along, following the trail like a dog on a scent. It leaves the ER and wobbles across the parking lot in front of the hospital. It jaywalks across Main Street, nearly getting hit by the 8:40 a.m. bus. It takes a sharp left into the alley and sneaks over to the dumpster behind KFC, keeping an eye out for the pimply faced manager with the bad temper. Lifting the lid, it jumps in, chows down with a quick breakfast of cold chicken and hard mashed potatoes, and moves on.

A stop by the liquor store to resupply, paid for by collected bottles and cans, and then it's a beeline for the river. The trail hops the broken chain-link fence, half slides, half tumbles down the muddy bank, and just like that, it's home. Time to celebrate with a drink. The trail throws some wood on last night's smoldering fire and gets it blazing just as other trails return from their journeys, their scavenging, and their adventures. The ticket to admission is booze, and each new trail brings it aplenty in bags and backpacks and bottles.

You may look at the camp and see nothing but a mess—filthy blankets, a couple of used needles, an inverted shopping cart with three wheels. What you don't know is that those are all landing lights. They are signals to the other drunks and other druggies still soaring high. When the time comes and the wings fall off their heroin high or fortified wine blitz, the lights of the broken bottles will beckon. "Crash-land here with us," they call. "Crash-land here with us."

Should you be so inclined, you could climb over the guard rail and down the embankment. You could stomp into one of their makeshift camps and start kicking bottles—shattering glass, kicking ass, howling at the top of your lungs. But all you would get from the Stevens would be blank stares, confused swigs of boxed wine, and eyes as empty as the bottles scattered at their feet.

Yes, the alcoholics are ER people. People between the notes.

But they are not the only ones.

In room five there's Mandy B. She is an addict—a Benadryl addict. Yep, you heard me right: Benadryl. Two or three times a week, she consumes industrial-size boxes filled with the pink pills of antihistamine. Popping them like candy, she departs this world for her space between the notes. Inevitably, someone sees her wandering about the Walmart parking lot, walking in front of cars, picking at power line poles, talking to people only she can see. The police are called, the medics are called, and then like the prodigal daughter, she is brought back to her people.

The people of the ER.

She stumbles about the emergency department, her muscles herky-jerky like a turkey that is half decapitated and staggering about the barnyard the day before Thanksgiving. She tries to walk. Her every movement is a—stop-start, stop-start, stop-start, *stop!* Her lips purse and words slur, her giant pupils dilated like two black moons stamped into a beet-red face. She swats at spiders and snakes and creepy crawlies that only she can see as they skitter and scatter and melt back into the walls, into her skin.

"Go back into your room!" I shout as she stumbles out into the ER for the fifteenth time in fifteen minutes, blabbing about some bat or cat or hat that she saw spiraling out of her hand.

Yes, Mandy B. is definitely one of the ER people.

Don't get me wrong. There are other people here, too. What you might call "normal" people. People like you. In room eleven, a businesswoman named Shelby with the flu. In room six, a four-year-old girl named Tami with an earache. In room nine, a seventy-year-old man whose name I can't remember right now. He has pneumonia.

When these people look out at the world, they only see others like themselves. The ER people are invisible to them. If they do see them, they are a brief curiosity at most. An afterthought, like the dog with three legs that gimps past your house on a Tuesday afternoon. You watch it pass by and then forget about it.

But I don't. I can't. Not when I keep seeing them.

Anthony, for example. He's in room eight. Anthony is a coke fiend. And not the soda kind. I see him every other Monday of the month. The Monday that follows the weekend after his paycheck. The paycheck he spends on cocaine and prostitutes.

Lately it's been cocaine-induced chest pain that has brought him to the ER. His weekend habit of touching the sun has finally burned him. The scorched myocardium of his heart draws droopy

ST depressions across his EKG, the lines stomped down by forty-eight hours of coke, sex, techno, and chemical joy. Joy that fills and just keeps on filling his forty-seven-year-old heart until it creaks and groans and starts to spill its precious troponin.

"Try not to use drugs," I counsel him, and we both laugh. "But seriously," I tell him, "moderation in all things. Especially as you get older."

I know he won't change. He has already had one heart attack. One of these weekends will be his last. I will miss his spectacular stories of debauchery, his loony laugh, and the twinkle in his eye as he tells me in much too graphic detail of the twins he spent the weekend with at the Motel 6.

They come and they go, the people of the ER. Face after face, story after story, body after body. Each trapped in their own space between. Sometimes I wake up in the middle of the night and I wonder who is checking in and who is checking out.

So many people. So many compulsions. Sometimes I find it hard to believe that we live our lives. It seems more like our lives live us. We're just along for the ride, hanging on by the skin of our teeth as our days skid past, careening wildly back and forth down the road beside the cliff. A wheel slides off here, a patch of ice there, and then an oncoming semi just around the next bend going much too fast.

Take David in room seven, for instance. David is a Dilaudid addict. Dilaudid is a pain medication. Dilaudid is the opiate of the masses. Dilaudid is the opiate of David.

When I first met him, David wasn't one of the ER people. He was just cruising down the road of life—roof back, face in the sun, the road ahead straight and narrow. He worked at Emerald's Garage on the corner of Second and Main, fixing diesel engines. He had a pretty girlfriend, he had an apartment, and he had a future. And then one day after work, he dropped his cell phone on the kitchen floor. The glass cracked, and in a moment of frustration, he punched the cupboard just above his sink.

When his knuckles hit the pine, his life hit the curve in the road. Two of his metacarpals, the bones you feel in the back of your hand, snapped and bent like shattered pencils.

"It's also called a boxer's fracture," I told him as I splinted his hand. "You're going to need surgery to set the bones straight." He nodded along, feeling foolish for doing something so stupid. "It happens." I shrugged. "Just get it taken care of, and you'll be good as new." I told him to follow up with the orthopedic surgeon so that he could get those bones back like they belonged. He thanked me, and we parted ways.

Or so I thought.

Well, David didn't go to the orthopedist. Not at first. Instead, he took the pain medicine I prescribed him: Percocet, a narcotic. Apparently, some little light inside his head that had been dark since birth lit up when he took that first pill. That light was so bright that it blinded him to everything else in the world.

A week later he returned, the temporary splint I had placed on his hand filthy and half unwrapped. He said he had overslept and missed the appointment with the orthopedist. He said his hand was killing him. He just needed some more pain medicine until he could reschedule.

I unwrapped the bandage and took a look. His hand was a mess, purple and swollen. It looked like it hurt. There was nothing else to do except wait. So not yet knowing where things were going, I wrote him a prescription for some more pain meds, called the orthopedist myself, and set up an appointment for him the very next day. He said he would go. He said he would be there.

But narcotics are a funny thing. That second round of pain medication did the trick. It pushed him right out of this world and showed him where to hide, showed him his own private space between the notes.

The next time I saw him was three months later. He had lost his job, his girlfriend, and his apartment. He was living on a buddy's couch. Some part of him had decided that he loved those pain pills so much he was willing to give up everything else in his life for one more beautiful hour of opiate-fueled bliss.

The pain pills had run out, but a coworker had sold him some Dilaudid, an even stronger narcotic. Percocet was suddenly child's play. And then a friend of a friend introduced him to Dilaudid's hillbilly cousin, heroin. Now there was no more popping pills and waiting for the bliss to begin. With an angel like heroin at your side, you could fly to the peaks almost as soon as her needle kissed your veins.

Long story short, after more attempts than I can count trying to get him into treatment, David had reached the end. He had learned the hard way that each time heroin carries you to the mountaintop, she drops you further back down the valley on the rocks below. He now was at the bottom.

Two weeks ago, he had finally gotten that hand surgery. They'd had to rebreak the bones in his hand. I examine it. It's like a beached whale with scaffolding around it, the exoskeleton of the surgeon's external fixation hardware sticking through his skin, trying to realign bones that had spent too much time out of whack.

When David became a heroin addict, he stopped worrying about needles or hygiene or really anything other than his next fix. Somewhere along the way he'd picked up MRSA, a nasty drug-resistant bacteria. It's been having a heyday with his hand. He rests his elbow on the mattress next to him, his right fingers pointed straight up. His palm is like a giant's paw: red, angry, dripping pus—a hot mess, as we call it.

Now, ironically, just when he needs those pain medications the most, they work the least. Daily doses of heroin have washed away the opiate receptors in his brain like waves crashing on a beach wash away footprints. The pain meds I am pumping him full of do nothing but wander about his neurons, unsure where to go, unsure how to help.

He lies on the gurney before me, dripping sweat from the 103-degree fever caused by the infection. In half an hour, he's going back to the OR. All the hardware has to come out and the whole process has to start again.

I wet a washcloth and put it on his sweaty head. He doesn't look at me. He just stares at the ceiling, counting the holes in the paneling between the lines, trying to understand just what exactly has happened to his life.

"I'll swing by upstairs after the surgery," I say.

He doesn't answer.

That's OK. The ER people never do.

I step out of the room.

That covers just about every patient here, at least right now. The ER people are their own people, a tribe, like the lost boys who follow Peter Pan—if you gave each of them an addiction and a chronic disease. When they have nowhere else to go, they end up here.

With us.

The staff of the ER.

The other people trapped in the space between the notes.

Let me tell you about us: the doctors, the nurses, the techs, and the clerical workers who staff the ER. Not the ones that show up for a couple of months and leave, taking a new job somewhere else. No, not them; they are the normal people. I don't worry about them.

I am talking about the staff who come to this place and never leave. Who make it a career.

Take Tom for instance. He is the charge nurse today. He is in his late fifties, a short, balding, chain-smoking, nitroglycerin-popping Vietnam vet. After thirty years in the ER, he is also an artist in the language of the emergency department. He weaves more f-bombs and goddamns into a single sentence than most people use in a week. His language is so apt and so magnificent at describing what we see that I often find myself speechless before him. He is a true word artist, a maestro of the maelstrom that is the madness we call emergency medicine. Next time you see him, ask how the shift is going—or, in his words, "the whole goddamn show."

Yet, when he steps into a patient's room, he is the pinnacle of professionalism.

He, too, is an addict. Only his drug is this place. The ER.

One time we talked about it. I was in a bad place. Work was destroying me. The never-ending onslaught had knocked me down so many times that I didn't want to get back up. I just wanted to leave. To be done with it. To work nine-to-five days, weekends off, like the rest of the world. I was tired of being trapped in the space between the notes with the other addicts, halfway between Monday and Tuesday at three in the morning.

"You can't leave, Doc," Tom said. "Sure, you could try. Maybe you should." He popped a nitro under his tongue; most likely his angina was acting up. "But this place does something to a person. It gets its hooks into you, and once that happens, they ain't never coming out."

I shook my head. I thought I was different. I thought he was wrong, and I could leave. So I did. I took a six-month sabbatical. I didn't make it two weeks before I went into withdrawal. The world was turning gray around me. It became drab, regular, regimented... and worst of all, predictable.

Early one Sunday morning a few weeks later, I was out walking my dog when an ambulance roared past, its siren blaring as it raced to the ER. It passed close enough that I could see inside the rear windows. A medic was doing CPR and screaming something to the driver. It was just a flash, just a second of time, and then it was gone.

I stood there on the sidewalk, staring at the empty street where the ambulance had just been. A minute passed. My dog grew restless. An elderly couple strolled by, out for their morning walk. The man nodded politely; the woman smiled. I said hello, and they said hello back. They were clean, their skin bright, their teeth perfect, and their gait strong.

Kids played across the street in a yard with freshly cut grass and hedges trimmed tight. The sky was blue, and the air smelled of spring. The children's father sat on the front steps reading the paper and sipping his coffee. I felt rested. I felt normal. I felt terrible.

I should have been happy. I should have been at peace. But all I could think about was that ambulance and the medics crashing through the doors of the ER, screaming for assistance.

Two days later, I walked back into the ER, my sabbatical abandoned. Tom saw me, nodded with a slight smile, and let loose. "The whole goddamn show is falling apart today, Doc. We got people stacked up in the waiting room thirty deep, pissed-off family members in the hallway, administrators breathing down our effin' necks." The medic radio blared out, interrupting him. A code blue was three minutes away. A fresh string of expletives burst forth from Tom, and he popped two nitros under his tongue before storming off to get the trauma room ready.

Across from me, Mandy B. came half walking, half jerking out of a room and fell flat on her face, breaking her nose. She must have found some more Benadryl. Before I could react, Steven staggered out of the room next to hers and squatted by her side, swaying like a tree in the wind, the bottle of Mad Dog he had snuck in still in his hand. He rolled her over and gently slapped her cheek as he called her name to make sure she was OK.

And suddenly I knew. This is my place. I belong here. These are not just the people of the ER. These are my people. My tribe. My place in the world is with them, among the drunks, the druggies, the haters, the handcuffed, and the broken. It turns out that it's the space between the notes that makes music possible.

Somehow, we all ended up in this crazy mess together. But that's OK, because contrary to what it may seem like, we are not alone in our addictions, our flaws, and our madness.

We have each other.

We, the people of the ER.

The First and Last Blessing

I step to the foot of the bed and pat the mattress twice with my right hand.

"Go ahead and move her over."

The two medics nod in unison and grab fistfuls of the sheet beneath the patient. They fold it around her like a hammock.

"One, two, go," the taller of the two states.

They lift her up and over from the ambulance gurney to the trauma gurney, setting the patient on the trauma bay bed. They drop the corners and the sheet falls away.

An elderly woman in faded pink underwear and a ratty gown now lies flat on her back, chest toward the bright fluorescent lights of the trauma bay. She weighs about seventy pounds at most—a skeleton with a thin layer of flesh wrapped around it. It takes me a second to realize what I'm looking at: a body almost completely destroyed by cancer. Some malignancy has melted her away like a lump of sugar dropped into a puddle of water. What remains now are just the clumps, the last little bits of her; soon they, too, will dissolve away.

The medics step aside, and I step forward. The woman doesn't respond. She just lies there, perfectly still save for the rapid rise and fall of her chest. Both of her eyes are squeezed tightly shut, sunk so deep in their sockets that I wonder for a moment if she had them surgically removed after some awful accident. I place my stethoscope on her chest, and her eyelids flutter, answering my question. The woman's eyes are not missing; they are simply retracted more deeply into her skull than I would have thought possible.

I listen to her chest through my stethoscope. *Lub-dub, lub-dub—pause—lub-dub*...her heart stumbles along irregularly like a drunk with a peg leg on a boardwalk. At the same time, her lungs wheeze and crackle with every breath, the sound of air stretching lung tissue that no longer wants to be stretched.

I look around. A body like this is a warning. It sounds as loud and clear to me as an air-raid siren or telemetry alarm. Someone has pushed this woman's body into this state. She is too far gone to have done it alone. And whoever it is, it's clear they will not accept *No* for an answer, cancer or not. I glance nervously toward the door of the trauma bay. It's empty, at least for now.

I flip my stethoscope back around my neck and continue my exam.

She tips her head ever so slightly to the side, and her scalp shines in the fluorescent lights. She has no hair, and I notice that the skin of her head is covered with tiny webs of dark purple veins. They wind back and forth just under the skin like the cracks in a windshield or a frozen puddle of water. Prominent arteries throb over each of her temples. I could take her pulse without touching her if I wanted, simply by watching them pound away with each beat of her heart.

It's as if the skin of her entire head is too tight, too thin. As if she were dipped in water and as a result her skin has shrunken like cheap cotton around her. Or perhaps it's more as if her skull has simply grown tired of waiting for her to die and now is pushing its way out into the world whether she is ready or not.

She is a living corpse—if *living* is defined as just a heartbeat.

Over the years, I have seen life end in all sorts of fashions. All kinds of deaths. Some have a quiet sound to them that is hard to describe. The death is a bell that rings forth into the world and calls home brothers and sisters, fathers and sons, mothers and daughters.

They return to the family from which they came to celebrate a life well lived.

At the funeral, there are slideshows and stories, laughter and tears, friendships between siblings started anew, and great-grand-children who meet their cousins for the very first time.

The final gift of the departed is to draw the family close and bind it tight one last time.

And then there are the other deaths. The ones that wreak havoc in the lives of the survivors. When a family member dies with con-flicts unresolved and betrayals unforgiven, they take with them any chance for peace. Those left behind are stranded in place, left hold-ing the equivalent of a grenade with the pin pulled. Siblings go to war with each other, and in their grief they say and do things that cannot be undone.

As death nears, neurosis can rise like a dark tide in every family member. Judgment is lost. They begin to mistake more chemo, more medicine, more time in the ICU as a legitimate form of love, a way to make up for decades of neglect and unreturned phone calls.

The family members no longer see the consequences of their decisions. They fight like starving dogs fight over a handful of bones, trying to outdo each other with their demands for more tests and more antibiotics for Mom or Dad.

Things continue to destabilize, and soon we are calling security to pull apart the fighting family members. The ICU nurses start to dread coming to work; they know it's going to be another day caught in the crossfire.

But death doesn't care what they do. It comes anyway, on its own schedule. And what little tolerance the family members had for each other is gone in a bright flash the second the code is called.

It's a strange thing to look at a body and know what kind of death awaits the family. But there it is, written as plain as day. And this body before me, this tiny woman wasted away but denied death, has all the markings of a catastrophic end.

"What's the story?" I ask the medic.

"Husband said he couldn't wake her up, so he called 911." The medic looks down at the woman and then back up at me, his expression sour. "He's on his way in."

"She's not on hospice?" I ask.

The medic looks down at his clipboard as he speaks, avoiding eye contact with me. "She has metastatic pancreatic cancer." He clears his throat awkwardly. "Full code." He glances up at me and drops his voice to a whisper. "And just FYI, the husband is on the war path. We had to call the cops to keep him out of the back of the ambulance."

I look at the woman on the gurney and try to imagine her husband. She has to be close to eighty-five or ninety years old. The medic sees the expression on my face and speaks again.

"You'll see what I'm talking about when he gets here." He glances nervously toward the door. "Don't let her die in the meantime. He's not someone you want mad at you."

I nod and turn back to the gurney, wondering just what kind of monster is on his way in. By the looks of her, he had better hurry regardless of what I do.

I rip open a package of oxygen tubing and attach one end to the oxygen outlet on the wall. I hook the other end, the nasal prongs, into her nostrils and run the tubing up over and around her ears before tightening it under her chin. With a twist of the knob on the wall, I start her oxygen at two liters a minute. She doesn't flinch or react.

My nurse, Elle, slides a pediatric-sized blood pressure cuff around the woman's tiny left bicep and pulls it tight. At the same time, the registration clerk snaps a patient-identification bracelet around the woman's other wrist.

"Her name is Iva *Mik-hail-ov*." The clerk struggles to pronounce the name printed on the band. "Eighty-seven years old."

I nod. "Iva, you're in the emergency room." I lean down and speak loudly. "Can you hear me?"

Her lips move as if she is forming words and then stop. "Iva?" I gently shake her shoulder. She moans but doesn't answer.

I reach up and hit the blood-pressure button on the stack of monitors over the bed, cycling the cuff. It inflates on her arm, and a few seconds later, the monitor chimes out in distress. Iva has critically low blood pressure, low oxygen, and now a low heart rate.

The inflated blood-pressure cuff seems to bother her, and she rolls onto her side, curling into a ball. Her gown falls off her shoulder, revealing her chest. A double mastectomy has taken her breasts, just as cancer has taken nearly everything else. It occurs to me that this is what people from Dachau or Auschwitz must have looked like at the end of World War II. Yet there was no war here, just a body pushed by modern medicine to a place it was never meant to be.

I pull her gown back up just as a man strides in through the door to the foot of her bed.

"I am Fedor, Iva's husband," he says with a Russian accent so thick I can barely understand him.

I step over and we shake, his grip nearly crushing my hand. I see now why the medics called the police. Even though he is in his eighties, Fedor is a mountain of a man. He towers over me and completely dwarfs Iva. He is wearing faded Carhartt overalls, the brown suspender straps stretched tight by a barrel chest and equally massive arms. He is as thick as an oak with the type of torso that you normally see on an NFL lineman.

The smell of cedar mixes with sweat, and I notice flecks of wood in his hair. I glance down. Sure enough, three of his fingers are gone, two on his left hand and one on the right. It is clear what has kept him so fit over a lifetime of work. He is a tree man. A lumberjack.

A logger. It's not hard imagining someone like him chopping down trees that have stood since Christ walked the earth.

It suddenly makes sense to me why no one has told him enough is enough. Why no physician has refused to do more chemotherapy or another round of radiation on his tiny wife.

Fedor hooks his half fingers in the top of his overalls, the back of his hands disappearing under a bushy gray beard. He nods, as if daring me to go ahead and tell him that his wife's case is futile.

But first things first.

"What happened?" I ask.

He grabs the bedrails and looks down at Iva. "I come home from work and find her sitting in..." He frowns as he struggles for the right word in English. "Recliner." He shifts his weight to his other foot. "I say, 'Iva, Iva.' But she doesn't wake."

"What kind of cancer does she have?" I ask.

This word he knows.

"Pancreatic," he says. "Pancreatic cancer."

"Chemo?" I gesture to my arm like an IV.

"Yesterday," he says.

I nod, my face blank, hiding the fact that I am beyond appalled. Any veterinarian who did this to a cancer-stricken family pet would be charged with animal cruelty and have his or her license revoked. Yet somehow we have decided as a society that more medicine is always better medicine.

I look down at Iva. She should be on hospice. To be honest, she shouldn't be alive at all. It is a crime against her, a crime against nature, a crime against the universe itself.

How Fedor can look at her every day and not see this is beyond me.

"Blood pressure is critical, sixty-four systolic, Doc," Elle says. She glances up for a second just as she slips an IV into Iva's tiny arm. She is waiting for me to ask him if Iva is a full code or not. If so, we are going to need more hands on deck. Iva is sinking fast.

I turn to Fedor, nodding toward the door.

"Let's step out for a minute. Elle will be with her."

"No," he says. "I stay here."

I take a deep breath. It's not worth arguing over.

As if to make his point, Fedor steps around from the foot of the bed and puts one knee down on the floor next to Iva. He grabs her bicep, his huge fingers nearly as big as her arm. He squeezes it gently. "Iva, I'm here now."

She doesn't respond. He looks up at me and frowns before looking back at her. "Iva!" he says again, this time followed by something in Russian. She moans and flinches at the loud sound so close to her face. "Don't you give up!" He leans closer, half encouraging, half threatening. "Don't you quit!"

It's all I can do not to call security and have him thrown from the ER. But I restrain myself. He has a right to be here. I have to respect that.

I put a hand on his shoulder and gently pull him back. He lets her go. He stands up straight, still staring at her, and absent-mindedly rakes his finger stubs through his beard.

We step over to the corner of the room, the best I can do. I hope against hope that somehow I am wrong, and he will suddenly see that it is time to let her go.

"What's the plan for her?" I ask as delicately as I can.

He stares at me, his green eyes ablaze with intensity.

"What do you mean?"

"I mean that she's critically ill," I say. "She's dying."

I can do a lot of things to buy her just a little more time, but that time will come at the price of her comfort and ultimately make no difference. It will involve needles and lines and tubes and catheters. I could put her on a ventilator, put her on medications that will force her blood pressure up, put her on antibiotics and fluids and a dozen other things—at least for a while. These days, with modern medicine, I can just about always get a little more blood from a stone.

"If her heart stops, would she want us to do chest compressions to try and keep it going?" I glance toward the bed. The nurse is shaking out a warm blanket. I watch as she sets it gently over Iva's skeletal frame.

"She was fine yesterday..." Fedor says halfheartedly.

Clearly, she was not fine, but I keep quiet.

We stand there together, Fedor staring blankly at his dying wife. There is a solidness to his presence, a strength so great that it has never learned how to yield or admit defeat. But for the first time in some eighty-plus years, his inability to compromise has finally collided with something even more uncompromising. The result now lies panting on the gurney before us.

"What does Iva want?" I ask.

"Iva wants to live," he says.

His cell phone rings, and to my surprise, he stops talking to me and answers, speaking rapidly in Russian. He looks back at me, holds the phone to his chest to cover the mouthpiece, and grabs my bicep so hard that it hurts.

"She better not die. Not today."

I yank my arm away, suddenly wishing he were gone from here. One of the most unpleasant parts of my job, oddly enough, is forcing people to live for a family member in denial.

"You understand?" He waits for me to answer.

"I'll do my best," I say.

He frowns, starts to speak, and then stops himself. He puts the phone back up to his ear, turning away as if I am suddenly invisible. I watch as he walks from the room, his voice booming excitedly in Russian.

I would like to tell you that I stood up to him. That I refused to do anything but give his wife enough morphine for her face to relax and a quiet room for her to be at peace. That I was different from all the other doctors who had caved to his threats.

But I can't.

I, too, am now trapped in his willpower, just like Iva. But the decision has been made, and I have to move on.

I turn to the nurse.

"Set up for a central line; I'll call CT. Get respiratory down here. Let's try some BiPAP—if that doesn't work, I'll intubate her."

Elle looks at me with disgust and gets to work.

I tear open the defibrillator pads and stick them to Iva's back and chest. If she codes now, we can shock her. We will do CPR and everything else, just as Fedor wishes.

Maybe they've been married for fifty years, and this is what she wants. Maybe they've talked about this exact situation, and Iva begged him to do everything humanly possible to keep her alive. Or maybe I don't know what I'm talking about.

I glance behind me. Fedor is on the phone out at the counter, staring off out the window at the empty helicopter pad while he talks in Russian. By the sound of his voice, he is getting more and more upset. This is going to be ugly.

I turn to Iva. She still hasn't moved. She lies on her side now, eyes closed. Her breathing is just as ragged as before. Even asleep, her face is twisted into a mix of pain and exhaustion. I step over to the computer and order some morphine for her, just enough to hopefully give her a few moments of relief. It's not much, but it's all I can do.

I run down a quick list of what could be causing her unresponsiveness, her sudden decline. Blood sugar is OK, pupils are not pinpoint from too much narcotics, there's no obvious bruising from a fall, and she doesn't have a fever—it's just the end. I don't know what else to call it.

I order a liter of saline, and the nurse hangs the bag and hands me the end of the IV tubing. I hook it up to the IV she put in Iva's arm, twisting the little white cap to lock it tight. As I finish, Iva moans and opens her eyes, a confused look on her face.

"I'm Dr. Green," I say. "You're in the emergency room. Your husband found you unconscious at home."

She tries to sit up, to look around, but she's too weak. She collapses from the effort, closing her eyes once again.

"It's OK." I put my hand on her forearm. It's all bone under my palm. "Fedor's out in the hall."

I stare at her for a moment, trying to decide what to do.

"Iva." I lower myself to a squat so that we are eye to eye. "Iva," I say again, louder. She opens her eyes. "You are very sick. Your blood pressure is critically low." I pause and then add, "You are dying."

She nods her head. It is no surprise to her. People always know when the end comes, regardless of what others tell them.

"If your heart stops, do you want us to do chest compressions and put you on a ventilator to try and keep you alive a little longer?" I ask.

She mumbles something in Russian as her eyes lose focus and drool runs down the side of her face. Maybe she is too far gone already. "Iva?" I say.

"Fe...dor," she finally replies, her voice just above a whisper.

I look up and with a start realize Fedor is standing behind me. He stares at me, knowing what I am doing. I step to the side and let him sit on the chair right next to her. But I don't leave. I pull up a chair next to him. It is the three of us now.

To my surprise, he nods. "You go ahead. Ask again."

"Iva," I say, starting over. "If your heart stops, do you want us to do chest compressions?"

I hate to keep bothering her, but nothing is worse than avoiding this question only to have a patient code a few minutes later.

I gently shake her shoulder. "Iva..."

Fedor leans forward and suddenly speaks out in a voice so loud that it seems to shake the room. "Iva, did you hear the doctor? Tell him."

She holds out her hand. Fedor takes it in his. She speaks several sentences in Russian.

Fedor nods and looks at me. "She say live."

I don't know what to do. I have no way of knowing if Fedor is telling me the truth. But it's all I have.

Fedor sees me staring at him and shrugs. He starts speaking in Russian to me, his hands gesturing wildly.

"I'm sorry; I don't understand," I say. "Let me get an interpreter." We have a phone number we can call if we need an interpreter in just about any language, day or night. It means putting the translator on speaker, and it's not ideal, but it's better than this.

I stand up to get our phone just as Fedor's cell phone rings again. He jumps up and answers, as if he'd been waiting for the call.

I just look at him in disbelief. His wife is dying. She needs him here, at the bedside. Whatever it is, it can wait.

He squats down next to Iva.

"Keep fighting," he says. "Keep fighting." He storms out of the room.

Iva doesn't answer; she just lies there like a pile of sticks.

I give up.

She has fluids hanging, and after a few minutes, her blood pressure is up in the nineties. She seems to be responding slowly to the oxygen, and her saturations are better. Lab is here to draw blood. I have a few minutes before anything else needs to be done.

I excuse myself from the room to go check on the department. The ER never stops—not for this, not for anything. I have to keep the patients moving. My job is stepping in and out of stories like a bookmark randomly placed in a book. It seems I can never stay on a single page for long before I am yanked out and thrust into the middle of the next chapter, the next story, the next book.

As I leave, I pull the trauma-bay curtain shut behind me. *The decision has been made*, I tell myself. *She's a full code. Get over it, and keep going*. I can think about what it all means later.

My next patient is a man in his nineties with dementia. He is shirtless and shuffles barefoot into the ER in handcuffs and pajama bottoms. Two policemen follow him, their gloved hands resting carefully on each of the old man's arms. He had punched one of the certified nurse's aides at the nursing home where he lived, and as a result they kicked him out. There was nowhere else to take him, so the police brought him here.

It takes a good five minutes just to get him to sit down on the gurney so I can examine him. He is so fragile that I'm afraid he will fall and hurt himself if he becomes combative again. Round and round we go. He won't stop talking about the Japanese soldiers he swears he saw on the rooftop outside. He is convinced the police are working with them. They have come to take him back to a prison camp called Fukuoka.

A little Ativan and Haldol later, he is sleeping soundly. The police depart. The nurse informs me that the nursing home is refusing to take the man back. I call social work, and the never-ending search for placement begins.

I swing by another room. An eight-year-old boy fell in the gym at school and hit his head. When I step into the room, he is playing on an iPhone and eating Cheetos. Mom wants a CT scan done. After examining him, I explain to her that he doesn't need one—he's fine. She is adamant. She saw a TV show where a child died because he did not have a head CT. I explain that a CT is a large dose of radiation for a growing brain and that radiation is not harmless. This just agitates her more. She demands to speak with my supervisor.

It's turning into one of those days.

I'm on the phone arguing about the CT scan with her husband when our receptionist interrupts me.

"They need you back in the trauma bay."

I excuse myself and hang up, bracing myself for what's coming.

I didn't think it was possible, but Iva looks even worse. She is breathing faster, and there are long pauses between her breaths. Her heartbeat now races across the monitor at 120 beats per minute. The end is almost here.

Fedor sits next to her at the head of the bed. His forehead is dotted with sweat, and he looks like he might vomit. It is clear he knows as well as I do what is coming and that this is one fight he cannot power his way through by strength alone.

I set up to intubate her, sedate her, and put her on a ventilator. I'd been trying to hold off, but now it's nearly time. I call respiratory to come down and assist. Everything is ready. I take a moment to go over her labs in the computer.

As I figured, she is in kidney failure from dehydration, she's anemic from chemo, and her potassium is dangerously high. I pull up her chest x-ray to find that her lungs are riddled with cancer. As I'm standing there, a critical-value warning pops up on the screen: her troponin is elevated. She has had a heart attack in the last couple of days. She is a ship pulling apart at the seams, and water is rushing in from so many places that no amount of patching or pumping can stop it.

She gets worse. The monitor chimes. Her blood pressure is falling again. I hang more bags of saline. I start a drug called Levophed, a vasopressor. It forces blood vessels to contract and squeeze, raising blood pressure in all but the sickest patients. There are three lines draining fluid into her now as fast as they can go.

I approach Fedor again. It's all I can do to talk to him. But I try one more time. He barely looks at me or acknowledges me. He answers with two words: "Iva live."

End of discussion.

The nurse and I get ready for the code. She won't look at me. I open the crash cart and get out epinephrine, atropine, bicarb, and vasopressin. I choose an endotracheal tube that will fit Iva and place a stylet inside it. I inflate and deflate the little balloon at the end to test it. It is ready. I get out the big steel blade of the laryngoscope and attach it to the handle, pulling it open to make sure the light on the end works. It does.

As I work, I run through her blood tests in my head one last time to see if there is anything else I can do to push back the end. I have treated her elevated potassium and everything else that I can. I force myself to stop thinking about what all this means and what I am about to do.

I step to the head of the bed with my airway equipment just as there is a knock on the door.

Fedor is across the room in a flash. He pulls the curtain back.

A man who looks like a younger Fedor stands in the doorway. He is in his fifties.

"Dad? Can we come in?"

Fedor steps back and holds out his arm, directing him in.

The man turns behind him and speaks in a quiet voice.

Then the others come.

A woman in her fifties. A second couple, in their fifties as well—a second son, perhaps. Another couple and a lone woman in her fifties. Next come the thirty-year-olds—four of them—the teenagers, and the children. The room is suddenly comically full.

I step back, just watching. Normally patients are limited to two visitors at a time. But this is not normally.

Each person, regardless of age, enters, sees Iva, and steps back against the walls to make space for someone, for something.

"Well?" Fedor asks, his face suddenly even more anxious.

Everyone looks to the door. We wait. Whoever Iva has been waiting for is nearly out of time. She is almost gone.

Finally, a young man of perhaps twenty-five comes around the corner and enters. He is pushing a young woman in a wheelchair. She is the spitting image of Iva, only decades younger. Her face is pale, but her cheeks are flushed. Her hair is a mess. Held tightly in her arms is a newborn child, wrapped tight and white with a blanket from the OB floor.

At the sight of the baby, Fedor staggers like an oak struck by a blast of lightning. He almost falls, his hand grabbing the bedrail.

"Iva!" he cries out suddenly. *"Iva! You did it! She is here!"*

Iva shifts in bed, and her eyes slowly open.

The new father wheels his wife over to the bedside.

Iva stares at the shapes before her. I can tell she is struggling to focus. And then her expression changes, and I know she sees clearly.

She pulls herself up to lean on an elbow and looks at Fedor, disbelief written across her face as if she is waking from a dream.

He steps forward and raises the back of the bed, just a little. The monitor chimes that her blood pressure is dropping as she sits. I reach up and silence the alarm, in awe of what is happening before me, of the story I have landed in.

Iva extends her arms. They are tiny and withered away like the branches of a tree stripped of all its leaves, its trunk nearly torn from the earth. But not yet. Her great-granddaughter is placed in her arms.

Iva cradles the baby to her chest and speaks a quiet blessing to her in Russian.

For seven minutes, I witness the very end of life meeting the very beginning of life, face-to-face. Pictures are taken to capture the moment, but I know they are not needed. No one present will ever forget this, myself included. Hugs are exchanged. Tears are shared. Joy is everywhere.

For just these few brief moments, Iva glows. She has done it. She has held her great-granddaughter in her own two arms, just as she always dreamed. Months of chemo, of bedsores, of intractable bone pain and retching all night suddenly seem no more important than dust in the wind.

She has lived to bless one more generation of her children.

She has lived to share one more child's first sunrise.

She has made it across the finish line.

And then it is time.

The clock does not stop. Not even for this.

We can all see it, and Iva can feel it.

She passes the baby back to her granddaughter. One by one, the family hugs her, saying good-bye. She kisses each one of them on the forehead and in between gasps whispers a final blessing in Russian for each of them.

One by one, they leave the room until it is only Fedor, Iva, Elle, and me.

He sits down next to her, and the giant man, the tree man, cries. His whole frame shakes with relief, with joy at what they have done together and at the quiet sadness of what has come at last.

I stand back, my silence a sign of respect, of awe. I was wrong about Fedor. Wrong about their marriage. But not anymore.

Fedor and Iva speak to each other in Russian. I don't know how, but I understand them. She is thanking him, thanking him for getting her to the finish line. It was his strength, his refusal to yield, his will-power that carried her when she had no more willpower of her own.

I look away—this is not my moment.

He kisses her forehead and whispers the same blessing she has given the others. It is the first and the last blessing. He glances up at me, and his face tells me she is no longer a full code.

He has fulfilled his promise to her, just as she knew he would.

She is free to go now.

Iva sits back and closes her eyes one last time. The grimace is gone, replaced instead with the quiet light of peace.

Almost immediately, her heart rate slows on the monitor above her. A few more beats stagger across the telemetry screen, and then the last beat sprouts wings and flies away, leaving the flat line across the monitor as empty as the body she has now left behind.

I reach up and turn it off.

Fedor sits next to the bed and stares out the window, still holding her hand.

The rain dots the glass.

In the distance, the mountaintops peek through the fog.

Iva's story has ended.

Sutures

The laceration runs along the underside of her left forearm: a defensive wound. The white cotton bandage wound tight by the medic still covers it, but the red stains soaking through tell me the cut is linear and at least five inches long—maybe more. I blink, and an image of an arm held up against an attacker flashes through my mind.

I introduce myself and step to the side of the bed.

"What happened?" I ask.

Delores Dominga stares straight ahead, her eyes as blank as the white emergency department wall behind her. Neither of us moves. It dawns on me that only her body is in this room with me—wherever she is, it's not here. Not now.

I take a moment and make a conscious effort to slow down: to speak slower, to move slower, to be slower. I sit down on the stool next to the bed, rest both elbows on my knees, interlace my fingers in front of me, and give the silence between us time to work.

I wait.

A minute passes. Neither of us moves. She reaches up and tucks her hair back behind her left ear, revealing her face. It's a mess. Her left eye is swollen shut. The flesh is purple and black, as angry as the fist that struck it. Just above the left eyebrow, blood has dried into a dark, leaf-shaped pattern. At first glance it looks like another laceration, but up close I can see that it is just blood smeared into an odd shape. She must have wiped her face while her arm was still bleeding.

"I'm Dr. Green," I try again. "One of the emergency room physicians."

Still nothing. Not even a glance.

"The medics said your arm is pretty bad," I say. I pause for a second. "Is it OK if I take a look at it?"

She lifts her arm straight out in front of her and then rotates it to the side in a robotic movement, bandage and all.

I wheel forward on the stool to get closer to the bed and take her arm carefully in my hands, avoiding the bandage. I peel back the dressing at her wrist and check her pulses distal to the wound. They're both strong.

"Can you still wiggle your fingers?" I ask.

She wiggles her fingers silently.

"All right, good," I say, relieved that whatever is under the bandage most likely didn't do any permanent damage. "Give me a second to set up my stuff, and then I'll unwrap it and take a look."

She bends her arm at the elbow and rests it back across her chest.

I swivel on my stool and remove the box of suture equipment from the drawer behind me. I tear open the clear plastic bag and remove the cardboard box full of disposable tools, setting it on top of the counter. I find the sterile blue drape in the bag and with a shake set it on the little tray next to the bed.

Now I take out the suture tools, setting them side by side before me on the tray. There's a needle holder that looks like a pair of small, delicate pliers, tissue pickups—which are really just fancy tweezers—scissors for cutting thread and tissue, and finally four packages of 4–0 black nylon sutures: thread with a curved needle attached to the end.

I ask again. "What happened?"

This time, she answers. "I fell."

I wait for her to elaborate, but she does not.

I nod. So be it. I look her over for other injuries as I continue to set up to suture. She is in her midforties and somewhat heavyset.

Her hair is straight, shiny, and black. As is the fashion among many Hispanic women here, she has shaved off both eyebrows and painted them back on with black eyeliner, the ends drawing to knifelike points.

She reaches up with her good arm and gently walks the pads of her fingertips over her swollen left eye. Between her first finger and thumb are three tiny dots: tattoos that signify gang membership at some point in her past. As she touches her disfigured face, her already blank expression somehow grows more absent. I can sense her retreating away, further inside herself.

"Are you hurt anywhere besides your arm?" I ask.

She shakes her head no.

I adjust the tray with the suture equipment so that it is right next to her arm. I pick up a brown bottle of betadine and flip open the top. With a squeeze, it squirts into a small silver basin a nurse has left out on the tray for me. I set a handful of fresh cotton bandages next to it.

Still, Delores does not move, does not blink. She is frozen. Domestic abuse cases are some of the most challenging I face. An inverted view of reality has often been beaten into the victims; they protect their abusers at all costs and see the rest of the world as a threat. They are often beyond my reach no matter what I do, long since abducted to a distant place by an abuser I will never meet.

Delores clears her throat, making a gold chain necklace with a tiny locket jump. I notice that the skin underneath is covered with tiny abrasions, the same width and shape as the links of the chain. It takes my eyes a second, but I can see a pattern emerging just above the marks: fingerprint-shaped bruises are forming on her neck. At the moment they're just barely visible, like day old wolf tracks in hard-packed dirt. Soon they'll be covered and denied, hidden away from the world under a tall collar or concealing turtleneck.

"When you fell, did you hurt your neck?" I ask.

She shakes her head no and answers with a tear. It drains from her swollen and smashed face, working its way down over a purple cheekbone before she swats it away with her good arm, her blank expression suddenly replaced by a mixture of rage and sadness.

"All right," I say. "I'm ready. Let's take a look at your arm." She rests her arm next to me on the tray. I gently extend it and begin to unwrap it. I note that the medics did a nice job when they bandaged it. It has stopped bleeding. Round and round I peel it away, searching for the wound underneath. Out past the bandage, her index, middle, and ring fingernails are broken, halfway ripped off. Someone in this town most likely has three deep scratches across his face.

The last few wraps of the bandage are dried and stuck to the laceration. She flinches slightly with each tug of the cotton. It takes me a minute, but by wiggling it slowly back and forth, I can get it to come off without too much pain.

The laceration underneath is perfectly straight, almost surgical. It runs nearly the entire underside of her arm, slicing a heart-shaped tattoo clean into half. The name Ricardo, which had been in the center of the tattooed heart, is now "Ric" and "ardo," each an inch apart. The edges of the wound are too smooth, too perfect. Only one thing does this. I am looking at a knife wound. Someone has tried to kill her.

"What did you fall on?" I ask again.

"The ground," she states defiantly.

I nod.

I pick up a ten-milliliter syringe with a big needle on the end. I plunge it into the little bottle of lidocaine and draw back, holding it upside down. A stream of clear anesthetic fills the syringe.

"Is that the needle you're going to use?" she asks, suddenly appearing interested in what I'm doing.

"No," I say, unscrewing the big nineteen-gauge needle and tossing it in the sharps container. "I use a bigger one to draw out the numbing medication. It takes forever if I use a small one, like trying to sip a cold milkshake through a tiny straw."

As she watches, I screw on a long, thin needle. "This is the one I'll use to inject the numbing medicine." The thirty-gauge needle is barely wider than a human hair. She instinctively pulls her arm away from me, holding it out over herself. It drips blood onto her jeans, but they're already stained dark red. The corners of her mouth turn down ever so slightly.

"It's OK," I say quietly, lowering the needle out of sight. "I'll go really slow; it won't hurt. It's only painful if the medicine is injected fast."

She stares at me for a moment before looking back at the gaping wound in her arm and then presses her lips together and takes a deep breath. She moves her arm back across the tray in front of me and looks away.

I aim the syringe straight up and give it a shake. Tiny bubbles rise and form into a pocket of air at the top. I depress the plunger, and the bubbles disappear before a tiny stream of fluid squirts in an arc through the air.

"Are you allergic to anything?" I ask.

She shakes her head no.

"OK. Hold real still, and try not to tense up," I say. "I won't do anything without telling you first. This is the worst part; just a little poke."

I quickly slide the needle into the wound, and she flinches but holds still. I inject. Injections through the surface of the skin hurt— that's where the nerves are; injecting through the underside of the wound up to just beneath the skin makes things much less painful. I take my time and inject slowly so that it won't sting.

She leans back and relaxes a little bit, closing her eyes, clearly relieved that it was not as bad as she'd anticipated.

"I see a lot of women who fall," I say.

Delores snorts and opens her eyes. She stares at me for a moment to see if I'm kidding or just clueless.

"Do you fall a lot?" I ask as I inject along one side of the wound.

I see it dawn on her what I'm asking. She's quiet for a moment, and then she answers in almost a whisper: "No, not as much as I used to."

I wait.

Without any prompting, she adds, "The kids get upset if they see me fall. They tell their uncle, and that puts a stop to it—at least for a while."

I finish injecting the wound and set the empty syringe down on the tray. I take out several big white towels, keeping them folded. She lifts her arm. I tuck the towels underneath her elbow so that the wound is directly over the center of the towels.

I pick up a bottle of saline with what looks like a clear spray skirt on the end of it. I invert it and hold it over the wound. I squeeze the bottle, and saline sprays out, washing clotted blood away from the edges and surface.

"How many kids do you have?" I ask.

"Three," she answers, staring down at the long opening in her arm.

"I have a daughter and two sons," I offer.

Her face softens, and she looks up. "You're lucky, Doctor. I wish I had a daughter. I have three boys. I love them all, but still, I wish I had a girl—someone to share pretty things with. Dresses and flowers—you know. Woman things."

I squeeze the saline bottle again, and we both watch as what looks like a miniature showerhead sends out fifteen little jets of saline into the wound. She flinches as the cold liquid hits the gash before she realizes that it's numb.

"It doesn't hurt," she says with a relieved sigh.

"Good," I answer.

The saline now sprays deeply into the wound, cleansing it. Pink liquid runs down her arm, staining the towel I had set underneath.

"How old are your children, Doctor?" she asks.

"Twelve, ten, and eight. All even numbers this year." I pick up a cotton four-by-four and dab the wound before gently opening it, checking the bottom of the laceration to make sure it doesn't go too deep or touch any big vessels or nerves. It doesn't.

"And your boys?" I ask.

She watches me wash her arm. "Jorge is twenty now, Jose is nineteen, and Ricardo Jr. just turned four." She flashes a smile for the first time. She has bright white teeth, almost all of which have been capped in gold. "Lord, was he a surprise."

I chuckle. "Funny how life happens sometimes."

She nods.

I set down the bottle and take off my gloves. I flip open a package of new sterile gloves and set them on the silver tray before putting them on. I dip a cotton four-by-four into the betadine. It instantly soaks from white to purple with the cleanser. I give it a squeeze before cleaning the edges of the wound and the skin around it, painting her arm a deep brown, hiding the tattoos underneath.

"Four is a fun age," I say. "Exhausting, but fun."

She laughs. "Yes. Ricardo Jr. is never still. He reminds me so much of his father already." Her voice fades away, and her face falls.

I pick up the needle holder and clamp it on to one of the 4–0 suture needles. I lift it straight up, pulling it free from the package. It hangs from the instrument before us like a long black hair from a horse's tail. We both stare at it for a second.

"Did you lose consciousness when you fell?" I ask.

She looks at me. "No, I didn't hit my head."

I glance at the choke marks on her neck, and I let her see me looking.

She blushes.

"And your neck is OK? Does it hurt to swallow or speak?"

"No, no, it's OK. It was very brief," she says.

I nod. "OK."

I pick up one edge of the wound and feed the needle down through the skin. I pick up the other side and twist the needle from the underside back up through the wound. I pull the suture all the way through, save for a tail of about two inches. I tie half a knot and pull it tight. As I pull, the middle of the laceration comes together, leaving two three-inch lacerations above and below the stitch.

I tie several more half-knots in the first stitch to keep it snug and clip off the extra suture. My hands move on their own, flipping and clipping, pulling and tying, drawing the edges of the laceration back together.

She watches, clearly fascinated. "You've done that more than once..."

I laugh. "Yeah, once or twice. Did that stitch hurt at all?"

She wiggles her fingers out past the wound. Blood drips everywhere. "No, it's all numb. It feels funny, but it doesn't hurt."

"Good."

I place several more sutures, tying several knots in each one. "When you fell, did you hit anywhere else? Your back or your stomach? Anywhere else you want me to check while you are here?"

"It's just my arm and face, Doctor. Otherwise I wouldn't be here."

"OK."

She sighs and sits back.

I put pressure on the wound several times to stop it from oozing so that I can see where to place the next stitch. When facing a long laceration, the trick is to start with the first stitch in the middle, splitting the wound into two smaller lacerations. If you start on one end and suture your way up to the other, you can finish with the two sides incorrectly aligned, like a shirt that's buttoned up wrong. I know surgeons do it all the time without any problems, but I'm an ER doctor. And, like every ER doctor, I've learned the hard way that in this place of never-ending chaos, simplicity and safety go hand in hand.

I pick up the edge of the laceration closer to her hand. I thread the needle through and begin again.

"Are the boys safe at home right now?" I ask.

Her hand clenches tightly into a fist, but she holds her arm still. I place another suture as she watches me. "Only Ricardo's left at home. The other boys have grown up and moved far away." She shifts her position slightly on the gurney and repositions her arm over the tray. "But he's safe right now. Ricky's at my sister's."

I clip the ends of a knot. "Was he there when this happened?"

"No, thank God." She sniffs, and I can see in her face that she's debating just how much more to tell me.

I fix my gaze on her arm; I focus on my sutures and let her think, working in silence for a moment.

"I can usually tell when I'm going to fall," she suddenly volunteers.

I nod without looking up. Much of what I do is simply giving people the space they need.

"I see warning signs in the days ahead," she says. "Usually lots of drinking, problems at work, or both. When the fight finally starts"—she corrects herself—"when I lose my balance, I send Ricardo Jr. over to my sister's for a movie night so he doesn't have to see it. She lives a few houses away. She understands."

"I'm glad Ricardo Jr. wasn't there for this," I say. She doesn't answer, so I add, "I wish my brothers lived nearby. You're lucky to have a sister you trust so close by."

Her fist unclenches. "Your family's not around?" she asks.

I shake my head. "No. My brothers and parents live far away."

She reaches across the gurney with her other hand and rests it on my arm for a second. I look up, surprised.

"So you and your wife have no family here?" she asks in a disbelieving voice.

This time I blush. I shake my head no.

"I'm sorry, Doctor," she says kindly. "How sad for you and your children. Family is all that matters in this life."

I look back down at the wound. It's coming together now. With a twist of my wrist, the needle starts through the next edge.

I stitch several more knots in silence. She'll have a long scar on her arm, I know, but it's starting to look a little better.

"My first husband never hit me," she whispers. "Ever. Even when we fought." She blinks back tears again, a faraway look on her face. "Ricardo was a good man—a great man."

I tilt my head, frowning slightly, wondering what happened.

She looks at me and answers my unspoken question. "He died in the fields. The doctor said he'd had a heart attack. He was only forty-one." She cries now, tears running down her face at the memory. The tears on the right are clear, I notice, but the tears dripping from the smashed side of her face are stained a faint red. I make a mental note to order a CT scan later. The tears drip down both cheeks, but she doesn't bother wiping them away or trying to hide them. "He worked himself to death. Three boys eat a lot of food, and food's not cheap."

"That's terrible," I say quietly. "I am sorry." I keep suturing, fixing the wound and drawing it shut.

She continues. "He was a great father to my boys. Gentle and strong. My older two boys, they're in the army." She smiles proudly. "They're soldiers because he pushed them to be strong and good men." A sob shakes her body, and I have to stop suturing for a moment while she regains control. "He would be so proud if he could see them now."

I hand her a sterile cotton four-by-four. She dabs her good eye, smearing her eyeliner.

"I've always believed that those who've passed on can still see the good things that have come about because of their lives," I say. I throw a stitch as I'm speaking. "Maybe somewhere he knows, and he's proud."

She stares at me. "Thank you. You are very kind."

She breathes easy, talking while I work. "When he died, I had a new baby, and I still had one boy at home—two mouths to feed. I tried to find work for a while, but it's not easy for a woman like me."

I listen while I work.

"So I married the first man I could find who had a job." She shakes her head. "Little did I know some things are worse than being single, even if you're poor."

I finish another stitch, flipping the knots back and forth on top of one another. Part of me is still thinking about the fact that my family is all far away. I push this from my thoughts. It's time to say what I need to say—I don't want to wait any longer.

"I worry that one day someone will hit you too hard."

She hangs her head.

"Hey," I say, putting my hand on her arm, "sometimes we all have to do things we don't want to do for our children. You did what you could because you're a good mother. *Because* you care. It just didn't work out. That doesn't mean things have to stay the way they are now forever."

She looks off into the distance, and I can see her eyes growing weary. She starts to talk, slowly at first, but each word brings the next, and soon the stories begin to spill out of her.

She tells me about her new husband, about the beatings, the rage, the constant threats of violence. She tells me about how he once woke her up by burning her back with a cigarette because there was no Bud Light left in the fridge. She tells me about the time he strangled her unconscious because dinner was cold by the time he staggered home from the bar. She tells me other stories, worse stories. She tells me until I want to run away from this world and the people in it and never come back.

Instead, I listen patiently. She needs to get the stories out—out into the open, out into the light. She needs to speak them out loud so that she can hear just how awful her life has become. There's a great power in stories, but only if we tell them, only if we share them. If we don't, they can become wounds that fester just under the surface, poisoning us and our lives with their power.

As she tells the stories, I can see her growing stronger. She sits up straighter. Her voice stops shaking; she seems to cross some invisible threshold inside.

I listen and stitch. Listen and stitch. Listen and stitch.

Finally, the moment is here. The moment of truth. I speak. "I worry that one day he'll hit you too hard, and your boys will no longer have a mother." I pause. "I've seen it happen too many times."

I pull the final part of the wound together and place the final stitch. The knife wound is now just a thin line on her arm, interrupted every centimeter by sutures.

"We'll be poor again," she whispers. Her arm trembles under my hand. "If I say anything, he'll kill me."

"No." I shake my head. "You're wrong. If you *don't* say anything, he'll kill you."

I tie off the last stitch and set down my tools. I am finished. I pick up the cotton roll and begin to wrap it around her arm, waiting for her to speak.

"What can I do?" she asks quietly.

I tread carefully. "I have a good friend here," I say. "Someone you can trust. Someone who once sat where you are now." I let my words hang in the air as I tape the bandage. I continue: "She's a nurse. But she's also a survivor like you. Will you talk with her?" I nod toward the door. "She's here today." And then I add for emphasis, "Now."

I can see Delores hesitating, and I worry that I've pushed her too hard; I've hurried too much, rushed the moment, and chased it away. It's happened to me before—more than once, I'm ashamed to say.

I hold my breath.

Finally, she speaks. "OK." She swallows hard. "I will talk with your friend." She reaches up and twists the locket on her necklace with her good hand, and her voice shakes with equal parts determination and fear. She has decided. She will tell her stories, I know, and by doing so, her stories will break her free from the one who has kept her locked away for so long.

I place her arm, now sutured and bandaged, gently back across her chest. She will always have a scar, but with time it will heal. With time, it will grow strong once again.

She looks down at her arm for a moment and then looks back up at me. I have other patients waiting: other lacerations, other problems, other stories. But for a moment, just this moment, I allow myself to sit with her and savor her decision.

Neither of us speaking, we sit together.

Delores Dominga and I.

Nathan

Three days before he was wheeled into my ER strapped to a backboard, Nathan James had a birthday. He turned ninety-four years old.

His wife would've made a big deal about it—she loved parties—but she was twenty-two years gone, dead at seventy-two. His son, had *he* still been around, probably wouldn't have mentioned it at all. From the time he was a boy, he had taken himself much too seriously and more than once had voiced the opinion that birthdays were a silly thing to celebrate and a waste of time when there was work to do. And there was always work to do on a three thousand-acre wheat farm.

Either way, it didn't really matter. They were gone, and Nathan was still here. For the past two decades, he had been the last of the James line—a leftover, a relic, a man from a generation that had all but passed on. Of course, Nathan being Nathan, he didn't worry about any of those things. He had a farm to run.

On September 16, at 4:59 a.m.—strangely enough, the exact minute he had been born so long ago—Nathan woke from sleep. He threw off his blankets, rolled out of bed, and stood up. The wooden floorboards under his bare feet were cold. It was pitch black, and the bedroom was silent. Without a moment's hesitation, he began twisting slowly side to side, stretching his back, getting ready for the day. The silence of the bedroom broke. Loud cracks and snaps filled the air as ninety-four-year-old joints remembered how to move after the night's stillness and sleep.

Twenty-five twists to the right.

Twenty-five twists to the left.

Nathan stopped. He squatted. He felt along the base of his bed. The warped floorboards of the farmhouse groaned as he shuffled sideways. After a moment of searching, his fingers found what they sought. He wrapped them around the smooth cast-iron grips, stood with a grunt, and started the next round of exercise.

One, two, three, breathe.

His biceps bent, his muscles contracted, his heart pumped, and he counted in time with each curl of dumbbell. Three sets of thirty. Three sets of thirty. Three sets of thirty...times...he frowned and tried to calculate just how many curls he had done over the years.

At thirteen his father had given him the York Arm Blaster Dumbbell set for his birthday. That was eighty-one years ago now. Eighty-one times three hundred sixty-five days, times three sets, times thirty curls. Minus the day Mary Sue died. Minus the day the barn burned. Minus the three days he lost after he rolled the combine and woke up in the hospital with a concussion.

One. Two. Three. Breathe.

He finished the last set and dropped the two weights to the floor with a double thud. It was too much to figure out in his head. He needed a pen and paper. *Maybe later,* he told himself. Maybe after harvest, when he was calculating bushels and pounds and prices, he would also remember to calculate curls and crunches and decades.

He lowered himself to the floor and sat down. Lying back flat with his knees bent, he hooked both of his toes under the bed. The hard floor pinched the skin along his spine. He ignored it. Time to do crunches. The old farmhouse floor creaked in time with each crunch and grunt. One of the dumbbells rolled over and pressed against his leg. He stopped and pushed it away, turning it sideways so it wouldn't roll back. He gave it a shove, sending it off into the dark, and resumed his exercise.

Nathan counted out loud with each crunch, his mind drifting.

"A strong body is the basis of a strong mind," David James had said to Nathan as they stood side by side, throwing hay bales into the pickup bed of the International. It was Nathan's thirteenth birthday.

Nathan had nodded and thrown harder, grunting like his father and twisting like a coil. With each toss, he had sprung loose like a striking snake, discovering a form of delight rising from strength and sweat and youth. He launched the next seventy-pound bale so hard that the entire pickup shook as if blasted at close range with a shotgun.

He threw again. The next hay bale hit the truck bed behind the cab and exploded in a cloud of chaff. He did the same with the next, and the bale after that, and the bale after that. He did it until finally his father stopped working beside him and just watched, laughing out loud at the brute strength of his boy.

Nathan finished his crunches. They were brutally hard at ninety-four. But now things got even tougher: three sets of pushups. He rolled onto his back and prepared himself.

"Effort is everything in life," his father had said as the two of them carried the bags of cement up the stairs to where the new farmhouse would go. "Effort is greater than strength, than intelligence, than who you know or what you know. Whatever you do, do with all your might."

Nathan had nodded. Even at fifteen, he knew the truth when he heard it. The next trip up, he carried two cement bags, one on each shoulder, 162 pounds total. He staggered like an old horse loaded down with too much gear, but he made it up the stairs and tossed the bags into the pile. His father had not said a word, but his eyes shone with pride. Inspired, he staggered up the steps behind his son with a bag on each of his own two shoulders.

Nathan finished the first five pushups and lay on the floor for a moment to rest. He could feel his heart galloping along in his chest. His body back then had felt as if it were made from a mix of light and steel, able to answer any question thrown at it with a fierce shout back. But not now. Now it could barely lift its own weight against gravity, barely whisper a response to even the smallest challenge. All that was left was grit. He scowled and pushed up off the floor with a grunt, ignoring the pain in his back, his elbows, and his shoulders.

Life is effort.

His father was right. He began the last set. One. Pause. Two. Pause. Three. Pause. Four. Pause. Five.

He finished the set and stood, twisting side to side again, trying to loosen up his back a little more. There was a lot to do today. Harvest started in three days. Late this year. *Harvest*—a chill of excitement ran down his spine at the word. He smiled to himself. He still felt it, every year, the same excitement he had felt when he was eight years old and his father had let him ride with a crew for the first time.

To an outsider, harvest looked like nothing more than the cutting of wheat. Like work and sweat and struggle. But though it was those things, it was also something else.

It was ritual. It was touching something bigger than himself, something that Nathan had never been able to find the right words for. He could only feel it and carry its mystery inside of him. All he knew was that his life was defined by harvests. He could remember the years when the earth exploded with wheat so thick that it was difficult to walk through the fields. Where the spring season felt so full of life he half expected to wake and find the barn covered in golden wheat. Those years the soil felt like if you tossed a stone into it, a week later there would be a boulder the size of a house. The soil was electric, supercharged, teeming with the energy of the universe as it begged to be released into life.

And then there were the years where the soil seemed to choke out every seed and insect that walked upon it. Where the dirt was so hard you had to kick at it with the heel of your boot in order to break loose a chunk. Growing wheat in those years had been like trying to pull water from a bucket of sand.

And through it all was the farm, the hills, the land itself. Nathan glanced at the window over the bed, cracked half an inch open. It was still pitch black, too dark to see the fields. Too dark to see the wheat. He didn't need to, not really. The rolling fields, the farm, the forests of grain that carpeted every square inch of earth in every direction—after ninety-four years, they were as much a part of him as his own flesh, his own blood. Maybe even more. Nathan could close his eyes and feel each curve of the earth around him the way most people feel the curve of their own shoulder or knee.

There was a lot to do today. He ran down the list of workers in his head. It took a small army to harvest three thousand acres. After breakfast, he would call Pablo, his foreman, and make sure the crew was ready to go when the time came.

He bent and reached for his toes, stretching. He needed to check each combine and truck today. To start them up and see that they were fully fueled, to make sure that the equipment was as ready as the men.

He took a step back, still thinking about the list. His right heel caught on the barbell hidden in the dark in the middle of the room. Over he went, falling backward, his nervous system's reaction time slowed to a crawl by ninety-four years of signals running up and down his neurons.

There was no time to react. Nothing to grab on to, nothing to slow the fall. He just fell. Nathan's buttocks hit the floor first, the full weight of his upper body driven into his lower spine and the old wooden floor below.

A Hiroshima of pain detonated in his lower back, pain so great that the world ceased to exist. A cry escaped his mouth as he fell back the rest of the way. His head hit the floor with a quiet thud, and he lay still. He couldn't move. All he could do was breathe, gasping loudly, trying not to drown in the pain.

Half an hour passed, and the shock of the fall slowly faded. His breathing returned to normal. The pain receded, little by little, until finally he could think again. If he lay perfectly still, it was almost bearable, almost tolerable.

The sky through the window turned blue. The rooster out back let loose, and the birds of spring filled the air with their early morning calls. The wheat in the fields dripped with dew, and the smell of wheat drying in the sun filled the air. Nathan breathed it in as he lay on his back, trying to figure out what to do.

Above him, bright sunlight worked its way across the windowsill and streamed across the bedroom, illuminating the unmade bed, the pair of unlaced boots on the chair, and the faded work pants and red flannel shirt folded neatly on the desk where he had left them last night.

It would be three days. Three days before anyone would come. Nathan stared at the ceiling and tried to think. Something bad must have happened in his back. He couldn't feel his legs at all. He took a breath and gagged. The smell of urine filled the air, and he realized that his bladder had let go. He swore.

Nathan struggled for a while. He tried to force himself back up through sheer willpower, sheer desire, and sheer grit. He didn't make it an inch. The slightest movement was agony. Each attempt left him worse off until he lay on the wooden floor, sweating as his back spasmed over and over.

Three days. Three days till harvest. No one would come before then. He tried to remember how long a person could live without fluids or food.

It would be close.

A dove called outside, the sound filling the room. A wave of almost unbearable longing passed through him, so strong it blotted out even the pain.

What he wouldn't give to have fallen outside. Out on *his land.* Where he could see the wheat and sky, where he could dig his fingers into the soil, and squeeze the earth when the spasms burned in his back.

The longing came again. It felt like one of the meat hooks in the barn had been swung into the center of his chest and was trying to drag him out the door to the fields where he belonged. To his land.

"I know," Nathan whispered to the fields. "I know."

This was no place to finish ninety-four years. Under a roof and surrounded by four walls. But there was nothing he could do.

It was too late.

He was trapped.

It was three days later when I met Nathan James.

"Ninety-four years old, found down, unknown amount of time on the floor." The medic counted to three, and we lifted the backboard onto the gurney. "Complains of severe low-back pain. Unable to move legs. No other history available." The medic stepped back.

I introduced myself to Nathan as I unbuckled the straps holding him to the backboard and dropped them over the side of the bed. He smelled of stale urine and stool and sweat. I put a hand on his chest, and it was cold to the touch.

"Nathan, you're in the emergency room," I said.

He made a guttural sound but did not move.

I looked him over, searching for injuries. His body was remarkable for ninety-four, long and lean, like an old greyhound who had never quit racing. If you threw a million bodies into the middle of the Sahara without food or water, his was the one that would stride out six months later, sunburned and grinning, unbroken and untouched. Seeing it strapped to a backboard covered in urine was like seeing a great work of art tossed in a garbage can. Somehow, I knew Nathan felt the same.

"Can you wiggle your feet?" I asked.

Nathan grunted aloud with effort, but neither foot moved. Almost immediately, he gasped as if kicked in the gut. Spasms visibly shot through his entire body, and his face contorted in pain.

I frowned, worried, and put my hand on his shoulder.

"Sorry about that," I said. "You can hold still."

He ignored me, focusing on slowing his breathing and wrestling the pain back under control.

There wasn't much on exam in terms of acute injury other than it was pretty clear he was paralyzed in both lower extremities. I wondered briefly if he had any idea of what lay ahead for him.

Stepping over to the computer on the counter, I logged in.

"Nathan," I said, "I'm ordering you some pain medicine and fluids. We're going to take some pictures of your back and see what happened."

I glanced over to see if he had heard me. If he had, he didn't acknowledge it.

When the CT scan was done, it showed what I'd figured it would show. His lower spine was a mess. The vertebrae, the blocks of bone that build our spine, were destroyed. The bones of our back carry the weight of our body upon them, and like anything with too much weight stacked atop, they can collapse.

When Nathan's buttocks had hit the floor and the weight of his torso slammed down upon his spine, the vertebrae below crumbled. Ninety-four years of gravity had left them thin and vulnerable. Three of them collapsed, one on top of the other.

After seeing the mess in his lower back, I ordered an MRI to check his spinal cord. When those bones collapse, they can rupture outward, the fragments crushing or even severing the spinal cord. Sure enough, there was a fragment that had clearly struck his spinal cord and damaged it. Nathan would never walk again.

His blood work was equally disastrous. The prolonged time trapped on the floor had caused rhabdomyolysis—muscle break-down. You might not think lying on the floor is dangerous, but it is. If you lie still for twelve hours, or twenty-four, or—God forbid— three days on a hard wooden floor, your muscles will begin to fail. The cells will become leaky and start to spill a toxic protein into your blood. That protein ends up clogged in your kidneys. Without fluids to flush them, they, too, begin to fail. Soon other systems fol-low, and your body slides closer to the edge.

I ordered a couple of liters of saline and some more pain meds for him while I paged the surgeon at the trauma center, ninety miles away. We sent the images of Nathan's spine electronically.

"He's not a candidate for surgery," the back surgeon said. "He's ninety-four years old, for God's sake. Stick him in a back brace."

I explained that he was a young ninety-four. A ninety-four that until three days ago had been more active than most forty-year-olds.

"There is no such thing as a young ninety-four-year-old," the surgeon chastised me. "I'm sorry, but there's nothing I can fix. It's full back brace, bed rest, and rehab."

There was more to the conversation, but that was the only sen-tence that mattered.

I had taken almost two hours to get all the studies finished and read. In the meantime, Nathan had slowly come around with the fluids and pain meds.

I pulled up the images of his back on the computer screen next to the bed. He stared at them without speaking or interrupting me as I flipped through the screens, showing him his shattered spine and explaining that he would never walk or use his legs again.

I swallowed hard and tried to sound positive. "We're going to fit you for a back brace and give the bones of your spine time to heal. You'll have to go to a rehab facility for a couple of months while we figure out your home situation…"

"But I'm never going to walk again?" Nathan stared hard at my face.

I shook my head no.

"You are one hundred percent sure about that?" he asked.

"Unfortunately, yes," I said quietly.

He nodded.

I waited, but he stayed quiet. "The ultimate goal will be to get you to a point where you can use a wheelchair," I continued. "That's going to mean…"

Nathan held up his hand, signaling for me to stop.

I stopped.

"Or," Nathan said.

"Or what?" I asked.

"The goal is to get me to the point I can use a wheelchair *or…*"

"Surgery's not an option," I said, repeating myself.

"You said that." A spasm came, and Nathan tipped his chin down ever so slightly and closed his eyes, gritting his teeth. He blanched. I ordered more pain meds for him and waited for it to pass. At last it did. By the time it stopped, his face glistened bright with sweat.

"I mean, what are my other options?"

I wanted to tell him that things would be OK. That he would heal. That we had all the science and technology we needed to do anything for anyone. But I couldn't. To this day, I still haven't figured out what exactly to do for an old man with a broken back.

"There's not really any other option," I said quietly.

He took a deep breath and let it out slowly.

"Can I refuse?"

"Refuse what?" I asked.

"Refuse it all. Refuse it and just be sent home?" He reached up and wiped the sweat off his face.

I shifted on the seat. I cleared my throat. I sat up straighter. "I can have the social worker meet with you and see if we can arrange for some kind of home visiting nurse. It would have to be round-the-clock care. It would—"

"You know that's not what I'm talking about," he said.

I scooted back. "I can't send you home alone to die, Nathan. If that's what you're asking."

He looked over at me. "So I gotta lie in my own shit for a couple of months until I die of pneumonia?"

The honest answer was yes. That is what we make people do in his situation. You can pretend that that's not true. You can tell yourself we send people like Nathan to a nursing home or, if they have lots of money, to a home with round-the-clock caregivers, pain medications so they aren't in pain, and Foley catheters so they don't lie in their own urine. But the truth is different. And the truth is not pretty.

I couldn't bring myself to say it aloud. I scooted back further.

"Why don't you meet with the social worker? Maybe we can figure out something that would be acceptable to you."

Twenty minutes later, Anita came down from upstairs and met with him. She spent two hours in and out of the room, making calls, taking notes, trying unsuccessfully to find a friend or relative who could take him in while round-the-clock care was set up for in home. But there was no one. Nathan was on his own.

"There's just no way he can go home," Anita said.

I swiveled away from the computer workstation as she sat down next to me.

"First of all, he doesn't have any insurance. His wife died a long time ago, and he never bothered renewing it. That means he would have to sell his estate to fund any kind of home care." She shuffled the paperwork in her hands. "It's almost harvest, so like every farmer right now, he has all this debt he plans to pay back when it's over. But now it's not going to be done." She shook her head. "Finally, he has no family. He had a son, but he died when he got bucked from a horse. If he had another family member around, things might—and I say *might*—be different. But he doesn't. He just doesn't."

I leaned back in my chair and drummed my fingers on the armrest.

"What's that leave?"

"I can get him into a nursing home once he signs over part of his estate to pay for it." She chewed her lower lip, the way she always does when she has something else to say.

"And?" I asked.

Her cheeks flushed slightly. "They really can't fix his back?"

I shook my head. "Not at ninety-four, with all his medical issues from the fall..."

She rolled the papers in her hand into a tube and twisted them tighter and tighter as she spoke. "He told me the one thing he has always feared the most is ending up bedridden and helpless."

I rubbed my face, trying to think of something, anything. "I'm not sure what else we can do."

"Hospice?" she asked.

"A broken back is not a fatal diagnosis," I said. "Well, in his case it is, but not enough in the sense that he would qualify for hospice."

The paper in her hand crumbled. There was nothing we could do, and she knew it.

She sighed and stood up. "Poor guy. Let me know when you figure out what the plan is. I'll help any way I can."

"Thanks," I said.

Back in the room, Nathan wasn't doing so good. He had dropped the nursing call light on the floor next to the bed. The spasms had started again, and being unable to call for help, he had tried to roll up onto his side in the hopes of getting some relief. He had ended up about halfway over before the spasms came with such vengeance that he ended up trapped in an awkward reverse curl, unable to finish rolling and unable to roll back. The sheets were soaking wet with sweat, and he was breathing rapidly from pain.

I grabbed his shoulder and hip and gently pulled him back onto his back.

"You're going to have to stay in this position," I said.

He looked at me with panic in his eyes. "Send me home, Doc." He forced his head to the right to stare at me, triggering another contraction of his back. "Stop all this bullshit and send me home. Have somebody prop me up out behind the house where I can see my fields and let me be. It's gonna be another chilly night tonight. At my age, it won't take long."

I tried again to explain to him why that wasn't the right thing to do. Why I couldn't just have the medics drop him off and leave him outside to die. Our conversation went round and round. He didn't care about ethics or laws or really anything other than the fact that his life was done.

As we talked, I thought about his CT scan. About the pile of bones in his lower back, his age, the fact that he would be immobilized in bed twenty-four hours a day. The months ahead were going to be ugly. He would likely get blood clots in his legs from immobility, and eventually they would break loose and spread to his lungs. If they didn't kill him, the pneumonias would. Little by little, they would slowly suffocate him. If he lived, six months from now he would be a shell of a person. A shadow of who he once was. At ninety-four, the body just didn't have much fight left in it.

Yet what could I do? What could anyone do? There were no good options.

"So if I go to a nursing home," Nathan said, "what then? Let's say I do all the rehab and stuff. How long till I can get back to the farm?" He paused. "Give it to me straight."

"A long time," I said.

"Like a couple of months?"

"Maybe." And then I caught myself. "But more likely not at all."

He looked back to the ceiling and didn't speak.

"I wish there was some way we could get you home." I rested my hands on the rail. "But not without a family member there to care for you. Not without round-the-clock nursing care already set up." I waited for him to argue again, but this time he didn't.

"Is there a phone in here I can use?" he asked.

I unclipped the portable phone from my belt and handed it to him. "Hit the green button to turn it on, dial nine to get out."

"Thanks," he said. "Give me a few minutes."

I left him alone and went back to my computer station. I called Anita. "Go ahead and get the ball rolling. It looks like he's going to let us send him to a nursing home."

"All right," she said. "I'll start the process."

Putting someone in a nursing home is no quick-and-easy thing. People often show up with family members expecting that we'll be able to make a call or two and find them a place. In reality, it takes hours of paperwork and phone calls involving social workers, insurance companies, primary care doctors, pharmacies, and others. It is a huge amount of work, and it's difficult to do from the ER because of the time required. But we do it anyway when it's necessary.

In the meantime, I continued seeing patients: a homeless teen concerned about a month of headaches, more likely from her eight cans of Pepsi a day than the brain tumor she was worried about. A fifty-two-year-old truck driver who broke his ankle stepping out of his big rig. I was about to see a baby with a fever when the nurse grabbed me, holding out my phone.

"The guy with the broken back wanted me to give this to you." She gestured over her shoulder. "He also asked to talk with you again when you get a chance."

I took the phone and thanked her, wondering where in the process of placement Anita was. Hopefully one of the nearby nursing homes had an open spot. I decided I would swing by and see what he wanted and then check in with her.

To my surprise, Nathan was no longer alone.

A Hispanic man in his early sixties stood by the bed. He held a sweat-stained and half-disintegrated straw hat over his heart. His thick, gray mustache sat on a sunburned face wrinkled tight with worry. As I entered the room, the man lowered the hat from his chest and stood with his arms at his sides. Even from the other side of the bed, I could smell diesel and exhaust on his clothes.

"This is Pablo," Nathan said.

The man lifted his hat and dipped his chin at the exact same moment.

I nodded back and looked at Nathan, confused.

"Pablo is going to take me in." He turned his head toward Pablo and immediately stopped, wincing from pain. Pablo practically jumped forward so that Nathan didn't have to strain to look at him.

"Ain't that right, Pablo?"

"*Si*, senor," Pablo said.

Nathan stiffly rotated his neck back toward me as far as he could. I stepped forward as Pablo had.

"Pablo here has been the foreman on my farm for about as long as I can remember. He's the only one who came looking for me. If it wasn't for him, I'd still be lying back there in my room." His voice softened. "He's as close to a living son as I have left."

Pablo squinted and looked away at the TV over the door. It was turned off, but he stared at it for a moment as if he were watching it. He cleared his throat several times in a row and smoothed his mustache with his fingers.

Nathan stared at me.

"You said if I had a family member, you'd release me. Right, Doc?"

"Well..." I hesitated.

"Well, Pablo's as close to family as I got. He has a wife and several grown children. They have agreed to let me stay with them while I recover," Nathan said. "I told him it wasn't gonna be easy, but he came anyway."

I stood, unsure of what to do. I looked from Nathan to Pablo and back again. Taking care of someone who is completely bedridden is a major undertaking. It's exhausting, even for trained medical professionals working in shifts.

"So you gonna sign off on this and let me go?" Nathan asked.

I looked at Pablo. Nothing against him, but there was no way he could know how to care for a ninety-four-year-old just diagnosed with paraplegia, let alone handle the sheer volume of work it would take to keep him alive.

"Can Pablo even get you inside?" I asked. "You do realize you can't stand or even sit."

Nathan frowned and spoke rapidly to Pablo in Spanish. Pablo replied, nodding rapidly. Back and forth, they talked in rapid succession. Finally, Nathan turned back to me.

"It's not just Pablo," he said. "Like I said, his whole family has agreed to care for me."

I looked up at Pablo, and he nodded in agreement. "Si, my sons help." He gestured toward the side of the bed and made a lifting motion.

"What do you say, Doc?" Nathan's voice cracked ever so slightly, the desperation just below the surface threatening to break through. "For God's sake, don't send me to a nursing home."

I looked at Nathan. He still lay flat on his back, in the exact same position he had been in several hours ago when he came in. We had taken him off the backboard, but now he lay in a form-fitting fiberglass back brace. It wrapped around him from his waist to just under his armpits, closing like a clamshell and latching in the back. Even if he hadn't been injured, it would have been impossible for him to sit up with the brace on.

"Doc, you gotta understand," Nathan started. "Three days ago, I worked out in the fields for sixteen hours straight." He licked his lips. "I finished rebuilding a D10 by hand, baled hay, and replanted twenty acres." He grabbed my arm, squeezing it tight. "I've never asked anyone for anything that I could do myself. But I'm asking you this, Doc." He begged. "Don't stick me in a nursing home."

I was torn. I knew they couldn't care for him. Nathan had no way of knowing what he was asking of Pablo and his family. But to be honest, I didn't blame him. I wouldn't want to go to a nursing home either.

Sometimes the best thing I can do as a doctor is to give my patients the freedom to try things their way, even when I know it will not work. In the long run, what difference would a couple of days make? Nathan's status was not going to change. Maybe after a week or so with Pablo's family trying to care for him, Nathan would see just how disabled he was and how much care he needed. At that point he likely would be much more receptive to going into a nursing home.

I pulled a pen from my pocket, clicking the top. "You're sure he's OK taking you home?" I said, hesitating. "It's not going to be easy for him or his family."

A wave of relief washed over Nathan's face. "Yes. Yes, I'm sure. He's as loyal as they come."

"Just promise me that if it's not working, you'll come back and get help."

"You bet," Nathan said. "If they can't care for me, I'll accept my fate. I'm not going to force myself on Pablo's family if taking care of me is too much of a burden. Once harvest is over, I'll be able to pay for whatever care I need." He actually looked a little excited. "With Pablo's help, I bet I could even run harvest from the bed."

I nodded along. Maybe he could. What did I know? What some people can do never ceases to amaze me.

I called Anita and let her know.

"You can't be serious," she said.

I shrugged as I said, "He wants to try it. I think we at least owe him that."

"But there's no way they're going to be able to care for him."

"Exactly," I said.

Anita was quiet for a moment. "I hope you know what you're doing."

"I'm just trying to help an old guy come to grips with where he's at."

We talked a minute more, and she hung up. I hoped that this really was the best thing to do for Nathan. That's all I wanted.

I began the long process of getting him ready to go. I signed the discharge paperwork. I wrote out prescriptions for pain medications, nausea medications, and medications for the constipation that would come from pain medicines and immobilization. He had to go on a blood thinner to prevent blood clots. We taught Pablo how to give the shots, how to empty a catheter bag, and how to safely roll Nathan to clean him.

I wrote out how much of each medicine to take, how often, and what to do if they weren't working. I wrote out specific instructions on how to get more if he needed them. I wrote out the orders for how often he needed to be turned in order to prevent bedsores, what foods he could eat lying down, what to do if he got a fever, got constipated, and even what to do if he vomited while lying flat on his back. I wrote out everything I could think of and then some.

My other patients began to stack up in the department while I scribbled away. I didn't care. This was the beginning of the end for Nathan. I wanted him to have time to make peace with what had happened. If being around a friend and his family made it easier, it was the least I could do. He was in a bad enough spot as it was.

I had a Spanish-speaking nurse copy my instructions into Spanish and read them out loud to Pablo. I then had Pablo repeat them back to her to make sure he understood them.

"Last chance," I said to both of them. "You guys sure you want to do this?"

Nathan looked at Pablo. Pablo stuck his chin out ever so slightly, frowned, and nodded. "*Si*, senor," he said. He was all in.

Nathan laughed. "Hell yeah, we do."

Finally, I wrote my phone number on a piece of paper and handed it to Pablo. "Call me, day or night, if something comes up and you don't know what to do."

He looked at the paper, folded it into half, and placed it in the breast pocket of his overalls.

"I'll give you guys a call in seventy-two hours to see how it's going. If something comes up before then, just bring him back. We're always here." I shook hands with Pablo.

"*Gracias*, senor."

It took a long time to get everything ready, and by the time I was done, I had nurses lined up to talk to me about other patients, a list of phone calls to return, and pages of blood work to review.

"Just a few more minutes," I said for the twentieth time.

Nathan and I were almost done.

I walked out to the parking lot as Nathan was wheeled out on a gurney, still flat on his back. Pablo's two grown sons helped me lift Nathan, once again on a backboard, into the back of Pablo's pickup. We put in a box of supplies, even a wheelchair for down the road—with instructions he was not to be in it until cleared by his doctor.

Pablo's sons climbed up on the bumper and jumped over the back into the bed of the pickup, sitting on either side of Nathan.

"How far is the drive?" I asked.

"About twenty miles north of here," Nathan said, staring up at me. "It's up in the mountains."

The engine started.

"If you change your mind or it's not working, just call an ambulance. We'll take care of you, Nathan. I'll make sure you get to a good place."

He smiled. "I'm going to a good place. Thanks for your help, Doc." He pounded the wall of the pickup bed next to his head, and Pablo started the engine.

I stepped back. The truck eased forward and drove slowly out of the parking lot. Nathan waved one last time as the truck turned onto the street and accelerated away.

The rest of the shift went by in a blur. I didn't have time to think about Nathan. I was way behind, and our wait times had climbed. I powered through the last couple of hours and finished up.

I signed out to the oncoming doctor. I was done. I grabbed my coat and headed out. It was a clear night, and the stars were out. Sometimes after a busy shift, I like to sit on the bench by the helicopter pad for a few minutes and gather my thoughts. It's got an amazing view of the mountains to the south.

I sat down and laced my fingers behind my head. I wondered how it was going for Pablo. Hopefully they would make it.

I stood to leave when Anita rounded the corner at nearly a sprint, scaring me half to death.

"They said you might be out here," she panted.

I picked up my bag and threw it over my shoulder.

"Housekeeping was emptying the garbage in Nathan's room, and they found these." She held out a stack of paper. "They called the nurse, who called me."

I took the crumpled stack of paper. My heart skipped a beat. It was Nathan's discharge instructions—the orders, the prescriptions, all of the official information about how to care for him. None of it had gone with him.

"What the..." I said, flipping through the pages.

Pablo wouldn't be able to pick up any of Nathan's medicines without the prescriptions. In fact, Pablo would have no idea what to do without my instructions. And they had left hours ago. He should have come back by now or sent one of his sons back to get the paperwork.

"Do you want me to try and call them?" Anita asked.

I stared at the papers for a moment as it occurred to me what had happened. I suddenly had the feeling the phone number Pablo had left us would be disconnected. Pablo, because he was like a son to Nathan, was going to do exactly what Nathan had requested. Unlike all of us in the ER, Pablo knew how best to take care of an old man with a broken back.

I shivered, glancing up at the sky. It was already getting chilly, and the temperature was still dropping. Tonight was going to be a cold one.

I thought about what Nathan had said to me when I'd first told him about his back. He was right. It wouldn't take long if he were left out in the cold. Not tonight. Not in his condition.

I thanked Anita and walked slowly toward my truck. I called the sheriff. He listened to my story and said he would head up to the James's place when he got a chance. Right now, he was south of town in the mountains with a rollover fatality, so it might not be before dawn. Somehow, a well-person check on a ninety-four-year-old farmer was not his highest priority. I thanked him and hung up.

I drove the long way home that night. Out through the wheat fields. Out along dusty roads in the middle of nowhere. I stopped at a random rise in the road and parked my truck off to the side in a field, sitting on the back tailgate.

The night was clear and cold. Nathan would be out in his fields by now. Pablo would have said good-bye and left. I could feel it. Somewhere, lying in the wheat, Nathan would be looking at this same sky.

He would lie there, alone, where he could watch the stars rise and the tops of his wheat sway in the wind, outlined by the full moon overhead. Alone, he would say good-bye to this world and make peace with a life that was at its end.

———

In the morning, the sheriff would find him, his wheelchair a few feet away. Pablo would insist that they had left Nathan inside, in his own bed, at his request. He would tell the sheriff that Nathan had begged for one last night alone on his farm and that he had only agreed because he had promised to leave with Pablo in the morning. Pablo's two sons would back up the story.

The sheriff would conclude that at some point during the night, Nathan must have clawed his way into his wheelchair and wheeled himself down to the field. Down to the spot where the creek makes a sharp turn and the wheat always grows thickest. Where the old oak tree rustles in the wind and each spring the deer give birth to fawns. He examined the scene and decided that Nathan must have wheeled down there and accidentally caught a rock, flipping forward out of the chair and dying of exposure during the night.

Who am I to say that's not what happened?

The sheriff later told me that when he found him, Nathan was lying on his back, his eyes closed and covered with dew, his face peaceful as if sleeping. He said it was the first time in all his years as a sheriff that he had ever found a dead body with both hands buried down to the wrist into the soil, dug in almost as if planted alongside the wheat.

Almost as if they, too, were simply getting ready.

Ready for the harvest.

Kurt

I put on gloves that are covered in blood.

They spring from the garbage can in the trauma bay, fly through the air, and snap onto my hands. Amy, one of the ER nurses, stands before me. Her face is pale. She is holding a blood-soaked towel, even bloodier than the gloves. She takes each of my gloved hands in the towel and gently wipes more blood onto them. With each squeeze and twist of her hands, the towel comes away cleaner and cleaner, while my gloves get bloodier and bloodier.

I do not understand this. The towel is now unblemished paper-white cotton. It looks brand new. Amy turns away from me and gives it a quick shake. The towel sucks inward, collapsing upon itself into a perfect square. She squats down and puts it on the shelf with the other white towels in the trauma bay. I look at my gloved hands. They shake violently, the blood glistening in the fluorescent lights.

I turn around. A man lies on the gurney. He is perfectly still, the color of death. A telemetry lead, a single green wire with a flat, white, round sticker on the end, hangs off his chest and over the side of the bed. It twists slowly back and forth in the air. Nothing else moves.

Back up above, a crumpled blue sterile drape sits over the patient's face, obscuring it. A plastic endotracheal tube is just visible, tenting the paper. It sticks out at an odd angle, the end of it attached to an Ambu bag sitting untouched upon his chest. No one is squeezing the bag. No air is being pushed into his lungs. I watch the tube for a moment. It just sits there. There is no rhythmic fog from his breath in the clear plastic, no subtle shift or curl of the tube as the man breathes, no sign of anything at all.

Whatever happened here is finished.

He is dead.

I stare at him, trying to place him. Has he been my patient before? I cannot see enough of his face to recognize him. There is motion in the room as other nurses, techs, even the two elderly ladies who work at the front desk walk in. But they all walk backward, as if they are playing some crazy game. I start to get angry. This is not a place or time for levity.

The ladies from the front desk shuffle backward past me into the trauma bay, their high heels tapping oddly across the linoleum. They do not make eye contact with me as they pass. Instead, they walk backward to the corner of the room next to the x-ray equipment. They step behind it and peer around the side, as if hiding themselves from the patient before me. As I watch, they turn to each other and hug, sobs shaking both of them. I do not know why they are here. They never come to codes.

Liana, the taller of the two, faces me. Tears race up her cheeks and disappear into eyes squeezed shut. Black eyeliner and mascara are smeared all over her face. The makeup comes alive and begins to move, sliding back up her face onto her cheeks and eyelids like lava slipping back up a slope. It stops where she placed it this morning before work.

Our biggest ER tech walks backward over to the man. One by one, he places his hands on the patient's chest and starts CPR. Or I think he does. Even the chest compressions are not right. I stare for a moment at his hands, trying to place what exactly is wrong. It's the chest. It moves as if stuck to the tech's hands. Each time he pulls up, the patient's chest follows, as if the skin is magnetically attracted to the tech's hands. Up down, up down, up down...the CPR goes like a flat tire trying to spin below a truck on the highway.

I am at the head of the bed now. The drape that covered the patient is gone. There is a hole cut in the front of his neck. He is too obese for me to see the underlying landmarks of the trachea, but I know from experience that that hole is an emergency cricothyroid-otomy—the last-ditch effort used to get an airway when everything else has failed. Doing one is the last-second equivalent of trying to jump out of a crashing helicopter the millisecond before it plows into the ground.

An endotracheal tube disappears into the hole of the cricothy-roidotomy. A respiratory tech to my left now squeezes the purple Ambu bag that is attached to the tube, attempting to blow oxygen into his lungs. But instead of air, each squeeze of the bag shoots frothy blood down the tube and into the man.

I try to yell and stop him, but for some reason I cannot speak. I watch in horror as he bags squeeze after squeeze of blood into the patient's lungs. He is going to drown the patient if he does not stop. I try to step forward, to tear the bag from his hands. But nothing on me seems to work. I am like an insect, trapped wide awake in amber. I am simply an observer in this nightmare.

I look down at my chest to see pink, frothy liquid spattered across my trauma gown and face shield. As I watch, it suddenly leaps from the front of my chest, the droplets racing through the air, coalesc-ing into a narrow spray, and finally entering the tube through the pressure valve on the top of the Ambu bag. I watch in dazed confu-sion. Tiny red drops now rise from everywhere around the head of the bed, like bees called back to the hive for an emergency meeting. They find their way back into the man's lungs through the tube.

All of a sudden, my arms move. To my horror, I reach forward and twist the emergency airway endotracheal tube out of his neck, working it back and forth and finally corkscrewing it out of the hole. Now he has no way to breathe. As it slides out, the blood and secre-tions covering it disappear. The tube looks brand new. A long piece of clear plastic packaging flaps up off the floor like a butterfly with a broken wing and swallows the tube in my hands. The fingers of my hand dance around it, and the package seals shut.

I look at the patient. His mouth is filled with blood. Now there is just a hole in his neck. It, too, is filled with blood. Air cannot enter or escape. He cannot breathe like this. A scalpel appears in my hands, and I dip it into the hole in his cricothyroid membrane on the front of his neck. I remove it. As the scalpel comes out, the sliced skin of his neck seals up perfectly behind it.

Now I feel myself struggling. My heart is working so hard it bobs my head with each forceful contraction, and my hands jerk violently with each beat. I am looking into the patient's mouth, trying to intubate him, but there is so much blood I cannot see anything.

I cannot find his vocal cords, his trachea, his airway. I need to pass a tube into his trachea so I can breathe for him, since it is clear he cannot breathe on his own. The tip of the suction tool is in my hand. It is set at full blast. It is in the man's mouth, squirting out more and more and more blood. I try to pull my hand away and fail.

As the blood squirts from the suction into his mouth, it disappears into his throat and pharynx, draining away to his lungs like a bathtub with the plug pulled. The basin on the wall next to me empties as the blood goes back into the man. *Well, that's good*, I think half aloud. *At least he's absorbing the blood somehow.* Then I catch myself— that makes no sense whatsoever.

The wall suction in my hand makes a whistling sound, and I see that its collection basin is suddenly empty. There is no more blood to put back into him. I relax a tiny bit. I am glad it has stopped; it doesn't seem right to fill his mouth with blood.

Around his head on the gurney, blood has collected into a puddle and covered his face. As I watch, it comes alive. Its surface trembles and twinkles in the fluorescent light, a tiny red ocean with a breeze blowing across its surface. It gathers on the sheet around his head and begins running backward up his cheeks and into his nose and mouth. I watch transfixed as it flows upward, against gravity. As it disappears, the man's face becomes clear. It is like watching a tide in the ocean recede to reveal a hidden shipwreck.

Oh no.

It is Kurt.

Kurt, my friend and coworker. Kurt, the nurse who's taught me as much about people as any mentor or physician ever has. Kurt, the guy everyone is hoping to see when they come on shift.

He is lying on the gurney, his face drained of all color. He is gasping, or exhaling, or maybe both. His mouth opens and closes, unable to give his body what it needs. His eyes are open so wide that they look as if they are about to fall out of his face.

Jesus, I need to do something. He cannot breathe. My mind races through algorithms and interventions that I have not thought about in years. None seem like good options. But right now, they are all I have. Some distant part of my brain notices that I can feel my own blood coursing backward as it races from my veins into my arteries. But now is not the time to try and figure this out. Now is the time to act.

Everyone is shouting at once. The room is filled with panicked staff. Kurt is the glue guy—the axle, the foundation, the cornerstone of our ER team.

Over the years, I have watched in amazement as the power of his personality has drawn other quality people to the ER. Sometimes a nurse will fill in for someone and spend the day working alongside Kurt. The two of them will chat as they work, as they care for patients. At the end of the day, the nurse will finish his or her shift and leave. And then, maybe a week or a month later, I will hear that that nurse has decided to leave the floor, or the OR, and come join our team in the emergency room.

When Jesus spoke of "fishers of men," I have a feeling he was talking about someone like Kurt. Someone who could cast his presence into a room and leave with a line of people tagging along behind him, all trying to be better people because of him. I bet Jesus could've used him. But instead we got him.

Except right now. Right now he is dying. There are two big sticky pads on his chest. Wires come off them and coil across the bed to the defibrillator. I watch as Kurt suddenly contracts his whole body and slams back into the bed as three hundred joules of biphasic electricity explode out of his heart and race up the wires into the defibrillator. It happens again. And again. And again. I watch as the defibrillator drains Kurt of his electricity, his life, his spark.

It is brutal to watch. Kurt is the best of this ER. He is how we imagine ourselves as caregivers, as doctors, as nurses, as techs. He spends as much time taking care of us on the staff as he does the patients. If it is better to give than to receive, then Kurt is better off than all of us combined. Because he always gives; he never says no.

It doesn't matter who or what or where; Kurt lives for others. Even when patients mock him for looking more like Chris Farley than Florence Nightingale, he wins them over with his quiet sense of humor and a sincerity that cannot be faked.

I hear myself shout in the trauma room. But none of the words make any sense. They are just garbled noise, as if the words have been recorded and are playing backward.

And then Kurt sits up. For a brief moment, I think he is OK. But all it takes is a look at his face to see that something is terribly wrong. He clutches his head, and his face is dull and blank.

I say something to him, and even backward, I can hear the fear in my voice.

His face changes, projecting pain instead of dullness. He lowers his arms from his head and sits back, resting against the upright gurney.

He starts talking garbled speech to me. There are telemetry leads attached to his bare chest. One has fallen halfway off and hangs uselessly over the gurney. I am about to fix it when it slides back up his sweaty side and reattaches itself to his right pectoralis. Kurt is trying to joke about something. He has that brave look on his face we all put on when we are scared shitless.

Amy holds out her hand, and a big syringe leaps out of the sharps container and into her palm. She walks backward with the empty syringe over to Kurt's side and attaches it to his IV. On the side are the letters *TNK*. It is the clot-buster medication we use for heart attacks; it disintegrates clots and thins the blood.

She attaches the syringe, and it fills back up, pulling the clear medication out of Kurt's blood and putting it back into the syringe. She steps back and puts the syringe into a package, which seals itself up. She runs backward from the room.

I am sitting next to Kurt now, on the stool. Sweat is pouring into him. Like raindrops rising into a cloud, the drops run up and disappear. His left hand is on his chest, and his eyes are wide. I have an EKG in my hands, and we are looking at it together. It shows a heart attack, a big one. I can't understand my words, but I know I'm telling him he is having a massive MI. I know he can read EKGs as well as I can, but I say it aloud anyway. I hear myself explaining—my backward speech somehow comprehensible now—that the cath lab is an hour away by air, which leaves us only one option. None of this is news to Kurt. He's heard me give this same little speech a thousand times before. Only then he stood with me, at the bedside, ready to help and do whatever the patient needed.

I list the risks of the clot-buster medication. I tell him that as it clears the clot in his heart, it can also cause bleeding in his brain or his belly. I explain there is a tiny chance the medicine will kill him, but more likely it will save him, will stop his heart attack. He knows this, but I tell him anyway. I speak to Kurt for the first time as doctor to patient instead of friend to friend.

Kurt is a big guy. All of us who work in the ER have our vices— our unhealthy ways of coping with the unhealthy things that lurk here. Kurt's weakness is Krispy Kreme donuts and junk food. I do not hold it against him. In fact, more than once I have brought donuts for him after a traumatic case or in a moment of great stress. We both know donuts are not healthy. But in the ER, it is hard at times to care about anything other than just making it through the next five minutes.

Kurt is the kind of colleague everyone wants. The kind of nurse every patient is lucky to have. The kind of healthcare provider who makes me want to be a better doctor. I have learned so much from watching how he talks to the drunks, the druggies, the conflict seekers. How he wins them over and befriends them simply by being kind. He is a teacher for me. He is a teacher for all the staff in the ER. He is an old soul, trapped in the most unlikely of bodies and unlikely of places. I strive to be like him, to be a light in this often dark place.

I stand up from the bedside and step backward over to the EKG machine. I feed the EKG back into it. It sucks it in like a paper shredder, and I step back to look at the screen in real time with the other nurse. I feel my throat constrict and my mouth go dry. I feel my heart pound and my hands tingle with fear. The lines trace backward across the screen, showing a heart attack.

I walk backward over to the bed. Kurt is looking better—a little more pink, a little less pale. He is pointing across the ER at one of the patients he was caring for a few minutes ago. I know he is asking one of the other nurses to go check on his patients.

His face is red suddenly, as if he were blushing. But the redness disappears just as quickly as it appeared. I sit down on the stool next to him. A nurse is taking the stickers off his chest for his EKG. She puts them back in the packaging, one by one.

Kurt stands up and puts his scrub shirt back on. His face is frightened, but he is making jokes again, just like he always does.

The scene changes before me, and I am suddenly sitting at the desk out in the hall, typing on a computer. I look up just in time to see Kurt bent over, clutching his chest. Sweat is dripping from the floor up to his head. He is greenish pale.

A patient stomps backward out of a room and begins yelling angrily at Kurt. The two of them stand in a doorway. The patient is screaming, berating him about the long wait. He is mocking Kurt about his weight. I am furious. It is a busy Saturday, and the man who is screaming waited almost four hours to be seen for tooth pain he has had since last Christmas.

What he doesn't know is that we've spent the day dealing with the aftermath of a head-on collision between two families on the highway. For a while this morning, the ER looked more like a MASH unit than the emergency department of a small rural hospital. Two children and one of the parents died. Kurt was the nurse for both children.

But of course Kurt can't tell the patient why he had to wait. Instead, he just stands there, letting the man yell at him. Letting the man vent and throw and stab all his rage and frustration at Kurt. Kurt just takes it. He has to. He speaks garbled words, and I know he is apologizing, apologizing for the long wait that was absolutely not his fault. He is a sponge soaking up the patient's anger, and I can see him getting saturated. So much of this job is learning to stand silently and let people rage at you. What you do with that rage is the biggest question every worker in the ER must figure out.

It is suddenly four hours and nineteen minutes earlier. It is sixty seconds before the car crash will occur on the highway.

I am standing with my coffee, getting ready to start the day. Kurt walks backward away from me, carrying a box of Krispy Kremes and putting on his coat. He walks backward out the ambulance bay doors.

The doors shut.

The doors open.

He walks in, suddenly walking forward, suddenly time moving as it should. He takes off his coat. He is here for work.

"Kurt!" I hear myself say. "I thought you had the day off." I look at the date on my watch. "What are you doing here? Isn't Jason turning eight today?"

Kurt takes off his coat and tosses it on the counter. "There were two sick calls this morning. Admin asked if I could cover. I didn't want you guys to have to work shorthanded." He flushes slightly, shrugging. "So here I am."

I almost say it. The phrases gather in my head, and the words form on my lips. *Go home. It's his birthday. We'll survive without you.*

But I don't.

Instead the moment slips away forever, gone in an instant.

Kurt holds up a box of fresh Krispy Kremes. "Plus I brought donuts."

"You're the man, Kurt," I say.

He laughs and gives me a high five.

He opens the lid and holds out the box. I grab a fresh-glazed donut—it's still warm—and take a bite just as the radio buzzes.

There has been a crash on the highway.

I wake in a cold sweat.

It is the middle of the night. That was more than a decade ago, I tell myself. Let it go. There is nothing more you could have done. My wife stirs next to me. "You OK?" She whispers. "Fine, just restless." I whisper back. She squeezes my arm gently and falls back asleep.

I try to hold still so as not to wake her.

Another hour passes.

There is light on the horizon now.

Eventually the exhaustion is enough.

I close my eyes and drift off to sleep.

The story begins again.

Jocelyn

All bleeding stops. All patients go. All stories end.

When I first began my career as an emergency-medicine physician, I found these truths to be irrefutable and self-evident. Like a newly severed spinal cord or the permanent brain injury of the drowned, no amount of my sweat, rage, or medicine could change them. They just were.

As my career continued, I began to find other truths as well. I didn't always know what to make of them, but I felt compelled to search them out, wherever they might be. They became handholds in the dark—places to brace myself. The truths, pleasant or otherwise, were at least solid and grounded, and because they were unchanging, they provided comfort within the chaos of the emergency department.

For example, I discovered that a patient has three paths out of the emergency department, and three paths alone: admission, discharge, or death. There is always a finite point at which a patient and I part ways—the point where our lives diverge.

I think about that point a lot: the final shared word, final shared look, final shared moment.

And then life goes on, and the patient I've cared for disappears into the past, mixing with other people, other patients, other problems. And that, I believed, was the end of that.

But a funny thing happens as you age. Doubt about settled truths creeps in. If you are so inclined, you begin to notice cracks in the building blocks of your world view. You start to experience brief glimpses of something bigger at play, something that begins to shine its light through the hidden fissures in your beliefs. It's like a small window at the top of a prison cell—if you grab the bars and hoist yourself up at just the right moment, you might be surprised by what's out there.

The first truth that shattered for me was the belief that when a patient and I part ways, it is the end. Sure, they may disappear from my thoughts for days, weeks, months, or even decades. And then one random day, my mind will snag on something, like the tip of an errant boot accidentally kicking a hornet's nest, and suddenly I am swarmed on all sides by memories.

A broken wrist here, a facial laceration there, an old woman dying on a gurney alone, a young man curled in a ball on his side as I put a needle in his back, a family without hope, a family with hope, a family no more. Facts retell themselves as new stories, new events, and new characters. Truths are broken and reformed only to be broken again. It is, when I really think about it, a moment of madness. But it's the only world I know.

I can never anticipate when or why or where it will happen.

It just does.

In fact, it happened to me again last Tuesday.

I was standing in the middle of a river when it struck. It was my first day off after a string of six shifts in the emergency department. I had woken up before dawn and driven out of town into the mountains.

Three hours later, I stood knee-deep in icy water. I was crossing a river, working my way across the bottom of a canyon. The plan was to climb the bluff on the far side and hike the ridgeline in search of elk sheds—antlers dropped during mating season last fall.

For whatever reason, I stopped midstream and looked around. Tall trees rose on either side of me, and the sun had a blue sky to itself—there wasn't a cloud to be seen. I stood with the water churning and surging around my legs, struggling to keep my balance in the fast-flowing water.

I turned so that my boots pointed downstream and leaned back against the current with my calves. I stood still, not really sure why or what had possessed me to stop. But there I stood.

It wasn't twenty seconds before a bright flash of red just beneath the surface drew my attention. I waited, thinking perhaps I had glimpsed a wayward leaf as it spun by, deep in the current. But then it happened again, and this time brighter. I leaned down for a closer look and froze. A kokanee salmon darted past like a bright-red arrow fired upstream under the water. A moment later another followed and then another.

I stood still and watched them pass, salmon after salmon, arrow after arrow. They did not know I was there. My feet grew numb from the cold, and I forgot all about elk sheds. I just watched them pass. They were fighting their way upstream for the very last time to spawn and die.

A small one worked its way up the current, trying to pass between my boots. It was slower and redder than the rest and seemed tired out. Without thinking, I reached down into the water and grabbed it. It was cold and felt surprisingly solid, like some kind of oblong calf muscle plucked from the stones of the river bottom. It thrashed about for a moment and then, to my surprise, stilled. Its eyes grew wide and confused. I had pulled it out of its life, out of the river, out of everything that it had ever known. Just for a moment, a brief moment, it was me and that marvelous fish glinting red in the sun.

I wondered about its life: where it had come from, where it had been, the things it had done, and the moments of its life that were unique and belonged to it alone.

I held it up higher, my hands dripping wet, and looked in its eye. Then, just for a second, I swear that fish looked back at me.

The stories in my head went wild.

———

Room nine: well-child check.

The letters turn red on the emergency department tracking board, signaling the patient is ready to be seen by a physician. I click on the name, assigning myself as the doctor. The letters turn blue: *physician evaluating.*

Well-child check is the triage nurse's code for a worried parent. I glance at the patient's age: four days old. A girl. Jocelyn Sky Gains. One by one I click the tabs on the top of the screen, flipping through her electronic medical record. She has no prior patient encounters recorded other than a brief note from the obstetrician who delivered her. According to his dictation, she was a term baby, pink and healthy, with an Apgar score of ten.

I open the next screen and scan the vital signs: no fever, heart rate normal for a four-day-old, oxygen level OK. So far so good.

I log out and head for room nine, draping my stethoscope over my neck.

"I'm Dr. Green," I say to the mom as I wash my hands at the sink. "One of the emergency room physicians."

She half smiles, her eyes tired and her face filled with the quiet fatigue of a brand-new mother.

"I'm Maggie." She gestures toward the bed. "And this is Jocelyn." In the middle of the gurney, a tightly swaddled newborn lies on her back, fast asleep. She's wrapped perfectly in the blanket, like a pink burrito atop the white sheet. Only her face is visible.

I sit down opposite Maggie, across the gurney.

"What's going on?"

"She won't sleep for more than an hour at a time," Maggie says. "She keeps waking up and then just cries and cries." A flush creeps across her cheeks. "Of course, now that I've brought her in, she sleeps like a log."

I quietly lower the side rail and pick up the baby. Jocelyn stirs slightly but does not wake. I place her gently in the crook of my arm and watch her breathe for a second, timing the rise and fall of the blanket with her every breath. Her respirations are normal. She is small, even for a newborn. I could easily hold her with one hand if I wanted to. I push back the top of the swaddle to see her fontanelle, the soft spot on a baby's scalp. On a sick newborn, it can be sunken or bulging; hers is fine. To my surprise, a few curls of bright-red hair lie against her pale, almost porcelain skin.

"She's a redhead," I say.

"Just like her dad." Maggie's eyes shine with pride as she stares at Jocelyn.

I unfold the swaddle the rest of the way to examine her. The air of the emergency department is chilled, and Jocelyn wakes. Tiny arms and legs jerk about awkwardly, controlled by a nervous system that is brand new and struggling to figure out how to work in this new place.

I carefully set her back on the bed and place my stethoscope to her chest. The bell of my stethoscope is cold, and both her eyes spring open. She cries out with a piercing wail that fills the room.

"Oh great, now you've made her mad," Maggie jokes.

Sure enough, Jocelyn lets it rip. She wails, blue eyes glaring out at the world as she tries to understand why she is suddenly no longer snug and warm.

I watch her for a moment. Her cry is strong, her breathing normal, her reactions exactly what they should be.

She is a perfect baby in perfect health.

For a moment, I wonder what will happen to her. Will she live a full life? Will she make it to old age? If she does, will she leave this world with a deep sense of gratitude and peace, or will she be torn from it, clinging bitterly to thoughts of what could have been?

Somewhere in the distant future is the answer. I stare at Jocelyn for a moment, trying to picture the life ahead of her. I know it's a silly thought, but for a moment I think about it.

I turn back to Maggie.

"She looks great," I say, raising my voice over Jocelyn's cries. "Her vital signs are perfect—everything about her is healthy." I hang my stethoscope back around my neck. "I see nothing you should be concerned about."

Maggie visibly relaxes, taking a deep breath in through her nose and exhaling slowly.

I wrap Jocelyn back up in the swaddle, folding and tucking it tight around her the way I learned when my own children were new. She stops crying and seems to stare at me for a moment before closing her lids and drifting back to sleep.

I hand her back to Maggie. We talk for several minutes about the sleeping habits of newborns. I reassure her that what she is going through is perfectly normal. She just needs to hang in there and have faith that things will get better as life with Jocelyn finds its routine.

I stand up. Maggie gathers diaper bag, bottles, and binkies before setting Jocelyn carefully back in her car seat on the floor.

"If anything comes up, day or night, we are always here and don't mind checking her," I say. "You're doing a great job. These first couple of days are often the hardest."

Maggie thanks me, and the visit ends. She signs the discharge paperwork and heads out the door, the tiny bundle that is Jocelyn swinging alongside in her car seat.

And just like that, she is gone.

I dictate the chart and head into the next room.

I stop cold in the door.

There can be no mistake.

It is Jocelyn.

She is four years old now, and her head is covered in wild red hair, curls and locks spilling about like half-coiled cables made from fine wisps of copper. The blue eyes I remember are scowling at me once again, tears glistening as she blinks and sniffs and fights back sobs.

She sits in the bed, her right forearm bent just proximal to the wrist like a half-snapped branch. It sits on a pillow in her lap, put in place by the nurse.

"I'm Dr. Green," I say. "One of the emergency room physicians."

"I'm Jocelyn," she says, her words stomping into the room. "My arm is broken. You need to fix it." She inhales and purses her lips, blowing out slowly, dramatically. "It hurts real bad."

A man who must be her father sits on the side of the bed next to her, his arm draped across her shoulders. His face is creased with worry, but at her words, he smiles. He looks to be in his midtwenties and has the same bright blue eyes. Wild red curls peek out from under a sweat-stained Seed Company hat, the tips bleached a faded orange from the summer sun. His face is covered in equal parts freckles and sunburned skin. He extends his hand.

"I'm Dale, her dad."

We shake.

"She was messing around on the hay bales," he says. "I told her to get down." He pauses, sitting forward to gently wipe several tears rolling down Jocelyn's face with the back of his hand. "I've told her a hundred times not to climb above the first bale." He shrugs. "But she already listens to me about as well as her mother does." He wipes his hand on faded jeans and puts his arm back behind Jocelyn's shoulders. "Which means not at all."

Jocelyn shoots him a glare that would make a teenager proud. "Kitty was up there. I can't just leave her."

She turns back to me.

"Am I going to need a shot?" she asks. "I hate shots. Hate, hate, hate!"

"I hope not." I sit down on the stool and wheel up to the bed. "I hate shots, too."

Jocelyn nods and bites her lower lip, trying not to cry. It is clear she is in pain.

"Did you hit your head on anything when you fell?" I ask.

She frowns.

"It's my arm." She points at it with her other hand.

"I see that. I just want to make sure you aren't hurt anywhere else."

She blows a curl out of her face, ignoring my question.

"It's not supposed to look like this." She points to the big bend in her arm in case I had missed it.

"OK." I laugh. "Well, we better fix it then."

The x-ray reveals a Colles fracture. The forearm is made up of two long bones, the radius and the ulna. A fall on an outstretched arm often results in the two bones breaking together. They bend and then snap, leaving the forearm looking like some sort of malformed dinner fork. It is a common fracture.

To Jocelyn's dismay, I have the nurse start an IV. But her arm hurts so much she doesn't argue. I lay out the fiberglass for a splint, and the nurse starts some morphine. Jocelyn relaxes, even though her arm is still bent at nearly forty-five degrees.

I walk her dad through what is going to happen next. He signs the consent form, and I trade places with him so I'm standing on the side of the bed with the broken arm and he's sitting on the stool. Everything is ready. It's time.

"Think of your favorite place," I say to Jocelyn. "This medicine we are going to give you is magic. It will take you there."

"That's not true," Jocelyn says, puffing a curl out of her face again. "There's no such thing as magic."

"Well, why don't you close your eyes and see."

I nod to the nurse, who hooks up a clear syringe to the IV and gives Jocelyn a dose of a drug called ketamine. Jocelyn's eyes grow wide and begin to jerk about with movements called nystagmus. The medicine is working.

"Whoa..." Jocelyn says, her face filling with amazement. "You guys are..." She sits back as her eyes go blank, her mind carried away to another place.

Dale stops smiling and sits forward suddenly, looking at me.

"She's doing great," I say. "This is what we talked about. The medicine is working just as it should."

He nods, sitting back a tiny bit but grabbing Jocelyn's good hand.

I pick up her broken arm. She doesn't flinch.

I wrap my fingers above and below the fracture while the nurse holds the humerus, the bone under the bicep, to steady her arm for me.

"One, two, three..." I pull the broken bones above and below the fracture apart, separating them. It takes nearly all my strength to stretch them. I use my thumb to push the edge of the fracture up over the lip of the broken bone. With a subtle click in the palm of my hand, I feel the bones pop back into place.

The hard part is done. Now I work quickly to splint the arm before the medicine wears off. I glance up at Jocelyn's face. She is still staring at the ceiling, eyes wide, mouthing words to something or someone.

"She's doing great, Dale," I say to her father as my hands work. I nod toward the monitor over her head. "All her vital signs are fine. She'll be coming around in a minute."

He nods appreciatively and squeezes Jocelyn's good hand.

The nurse and I work together to wrap Jocelyn's arm in a light cotton bandage. I peel open the foil package that holds the fiberglass splint and run it briefly under the faucet before drying it off with a towel. It warms in my hands as the chemical reaction begins.

I wrap the fiberglass, starting at the palm of her hand and running it down around her elbow and back up. It begins to harden in my hands as I work. Once it is the correct shape, I wrap an elastic bandage around the fiberglass to hold it.

I grab just over the fracture, add some gentle pressure to make sure it stays in place, and slightly flex Jocelyn's wrist.

"Ow," she says and then slips back to wherever she was.

I hold the wrist and bones in place until the splint is hard enough to do it for me. I set her splinted forearm down across her chest. It is straight once again.

"That's it," I say to Dale. "We're all done."

"Jocelyn." He leans close. "The doctor is finished." He gives her hand a squeeze.

She blinks a few times but doesn't speak. The medication still in full effect.

I flip off the lights so there is minimal stimulation and speak to her dad in a quiet voice. "Now we just wait for the medicine to wear off. If you want to talk to her quietly, it will help her as she comes around. A parent's voice makes it less disorienting as the medicine wears off."

Dale scoots up next to the gurney and whispers, both his hands now wrapped around hers. "There once was a little bear named Blueberry..."

I turn away while he continues speaking in a soft voice to Jocelyn. She is lucky to have a dad like him. I wash my hands in the sink and towel them off.

Over the next few minutes, Jocelyn wakes up.

"What happened?" she asks.

"We fixed your arm."

She holds it up in front of her, confused. "Is it all better?"

"It's on its way."

Forty-five minutes later, she can walk a straight line and is clear-headed enough to be safely discharged.

"I hope your arm feels better," I say as she walks out hand in hand with her father.

She drops his hand and high-fives me with her unsplinted hand. "Thanks." She flips the curls from her face. "See you around."

I give her a sticker, and she disappears through the emergency department doors.

I check the patient tracking board. Everyone is waiting for labs or x-rays or fluids—I have a minute to myself. I jog down to the doctors' lounge and search the fridge. As usual it has been picked almost bare. I grab a day-old egg sandwich and a bag of chips. No one is around because it's the middle of the morning. I check my hospital mailbox and eat in a hurry as I walk back to the emergency department. It always makes me nervous to be away when I'm the only one on duty.

If anything life threatening came in, I know my nurses would page me, but I hate not being there in the first moments. You never know when a few seconds would have made all the difference.

I get back to the emergency department, sign up for the next patient, and head on in.

Jocelyn is seventeen now.

Her red hair is shorter and has been pulled back into a ponytail. Freckles dot her nose and cheeks, and she is tall and lanky like her father.

Both her mom and dad are here with her. The effect of time on their bodies is striking. Her dad's hair has thinned on top, and both his temples are dusted with gray. He has added a few pounds here and there, but his eyes still shine when he looks at Jocelyn.

I haven't seen Maggie since Jocelyn was four days old. She stands next to her husband at the side of the bed. Her posture is not quite as straight as it used to be, and the lines of her face are deeper and more pronounced. Her wrinkles remind me of a picture frame, drawing out a painting's hidden colors and depths.

They stand together side by side, their shoulders just touching, both their faces creased with worry.

"Hi, Jocelyn," I say. "I'm Dr. Green, one of the emergency room physicians."

She doesn't look up; she just moves the icepack on her knee and grits her teeth. She is wearing an O'Leary High School basketball uniform. It's black with green trim and has a knight on the front, brandishing a sword and shield.

I sit down on the stool next to Jocelyn, and she looks up. She doesn't remember me, of course.

"What happened?" I ask.

"She went up for a rebound, and as she came down, she fell over another player," Maggie answers for her.

"I torqued my knee." Jocelyn ignores her mother's comment.

"Can you put any weight on it?" I ask.

She shakes her head. "I can't even bend it." She tries to demonstrate and blanches from pain as it moves. The bag of ice falls off onto the bed. She grabs it and slams it back onto her knee in frustration, her face flinching briefly before twisting in a furious scowl.

"They made it to playoffs..." her dad says, his voice fading away.

I nod. I understand that to them it is more than just sports— it is an essential part of who she is right now and who she is becoming.

I lift the bag of ice and examine her knee. It is swollen, and a purple hue is already forming along the joint space. It does not look good.

"Where does it hurt?" I ask as I carefully palpate along the joint line.

"It's deep inside," she says. "It feels like it's loose or something."

I put the icepack back over her knee.

"What do you think?" her dad asks.

Before I can answer, Jocelyn interrupts, cutting to the chase. "Will I be able to play next week?"

"First things first," I say. "Let's get an x-ray and see if it's broken. Then we can talk about next week."

She looks up at her parents, afraid, suddenly a young girl again.

"Let's get the x-ray like the doctor says." Her mom sits down on the mattress next to her. "Maybe it will be OK."

The x-ray is fine. With so much swelling, I was worried she might have fractured her tibial plateau, the top of the big bone in the lower leg. If a fracture occurs at the joint line, it can be career ending for a young athlete. But hers is OK.

I pull up the x-rays of her knee on the computer in the room, turning the screen so that they can all see.

"This is your tibia." I trace a vertical line down the screen over the bone. "The fibula is this little one." I tap the screen. "This is your kneecap." I circle the patella. "And lastly, your femur."

She nods along, impatient, caring only about one thing.

"They all look OK."

Now that I know it's not broken, I test for ligamentous injury. I stabilize her upper leg and push back just below the knee. The posterior cruciate ligament is OK. Now for the big one. I pull the lower leg gently forward just below the knee while holding the femur in place. It moves much too easily and much too far.

Jocelyn cries out immediately and covers her mouth with her hand.

"Sorry," I say. I gently put her leg down, placing the icepack back on top. "It's your ACL."

"So..."

"So no game next week."

Color floods her face.

"You need to see an orthopedic surgeon and be evaluated. You're probably going to need surgery."

Jocelyn pulls the pillow over her face and sobs.

I sit for a moment while she cries. Her mom and dad look like they might throw up. The season, at least for her, is over.

She's going to need surgery, rehab, and then who knows. Hopefully she will recover enough to run and ski and do all the things a young woman should be able to do. But ACLs don't always go along with people's plans.

The nurse puts her in a knee brace and teaches her how to use crutches. Jocelyn clomps around the emergency department, practicing while I move on to other patients.

She stops at the desk while I'm working on a chart.

"What's wrong with that guy in room five? The one on the breathing machine."

I lean to the side and look behind her into room five. It's a man who crashed his motorcycle, collapsing his lungs and breaking multiple bones. The trauma-room floor is covered in ripped-open packages, cut-up motorcycle clothes, and blood from when I put in his chest tubes to reinflate his lungs. A housekeeper with a bucket and a mop is cleaning up next to the bed.

"He was in an accident," I say.

"Is that his blood on the floor in there?"

I pause for a moment. "Yes."

She stares into room five, not really talking to me. "I guess I should be grateful I'm not him."

The nurse working in room five adjusts the ventilator and sees Jocelyn watching, wide-eyed. She stops and walks over, pulling the curtain shut.

"Thanks for your help." Jocelyn turns back to the desk.

"See you around," I say, giving her a wave.

She clomps off on her crutches, her mom and dad in tow.

Once again, gone.

It's strange how much of emergency medicine is beginnings and endings. How my shifts are filled with people who have played a sport for the last time, or worked a job for the last time, or even seen a loved one for the last time. On the flip side, it is a career filled with first days, not always so pleasant: first day of a cancer diagnosis, first moments without a loved one, first minutes wondering just what the hell happened to your life.

It's easy to lose myself in such thoughts, and for the millionth time, I remind myself of all the good things that happen here, too. I have to choose which to focus on.

A light goes on over room three—the next patient is ready for the doctor. I put my pondering aside and head into the room.

Jocelyn is twenty-eight now. Her hair is wild and curly once again. Her pale skin is white...too white. Both lips are a faded gray, and her eyes are sunken. The monitor goes off just as I step into the room—her blood pressure is 74/40, critically low.

A man stands next to her. By the look on his face, he must be her husband. He is tall and bulky with buzz-cut blond hair and a worried face. He bounces a newborn on his shoulder, anxiously pacing back and forth beside the bed. When I step into the room, he crouches and sets the baby in a car seat on the floor. He stands back up and extends a hand.

"I'm Jon," he says, speaking so fast I can hardly understand him. "This is my wife, Jocelyn. Something's wrong. I just know it."

"Start at the beginning," I say. There's no time for formalities. One glance and it's easy to tell she's in a dangerous place.

He starts talking, his speech so pressured his words trip and stumble. But he doesn't stop. "She was fine a week ago. Pregnancy was fine. Well, almost fine. She had diabetes toward the end. But the doctor said it would go away. Her blood sugars were all over the place. One was in the three hundreds. We were checking almost hourly at the end."

He continues to talk as Noah, one of the emergency-department nurses, enters the room. I watch as Noah's eyes go straight from Jocelyn's face to the monitor and then to me. I nod subtly, and he's gone. He's back in the blink of an eye with several big bags of saline tucked under each arm and two large-bore IVs. He wheels up next to Jocelyn and sets about getting vascular access.

"What happened this week?" I interrupt Jon.

Jon sits down next to Jocelyn, opposite Noah, and then stands back up and sits back down. He's all over the place. "She just had a baby." He stands back up and grabs the rail. "We just had a baby."

"C-section?"

He nods.

"How many days ago?"

"Three."

"When did she start feeling bad?" I ask.

"She was dizzy all day yesterday and then started getting weak last night. She said her stomach hurt. But she wasn't bleeding anymore, so we figured it was just standard stuff."

I nod and sit down next to Jocelyn.

"I'm Dr. Green," I say. "One of the emergency room physicians."

Jocelyn's eyes flutter, and she nods ever so slightly before closing them again.

I pull up Jocelyn's gown to expose her abdomen. The surgical incision is clean and looks as it should three days post op. I put on gloves and put a hand on her belly—her skin is cool to the touch. Her abdomen is distended and firm. I barely press at all and she moans in pain.

"Who was your doctor, Jocelyn?"

Her eyelids flutter again, and the familiar blue eyes stare up at me.

"Dr. Karnowski."

I stand back up.

"What is it?" Jon asks.

"She's bleeding inside."

He grabs his head as if it were about to explode. "Jesus, I knew it. I knew it."

I excuse myself and call Dr. Karnowski. He's a fantastic obstetrician with surgical skills to match. But even the best cannot always be perfect. Sometimes a suture slips, a scalpel nicks, or a tissue tears. That's just the way it is.

Twenty minutes later, she's wheeled away to the operating room, Jon and the baby in tow. I watch them go, wondering if this is the last time I will ever see Jocelyn. Maybe this is it. Maybe that's the end of her.

They are barely out the door before the charge nurse grabs me. "We got a bad burn, trauma room two."

I step in, and there's Jocelyn, forty-four now. Her pale skin is white, not the sheet white of anemia like before but the sheet white of fear. She is not the patient. She stands with her arm around a sixteen-year-old boy, a younger image of her husband, Jon.

Jon is on the gurney, except now I hardly recognize him. He is covered in black soot and the smell of burned flesh fills the room. A medic squeezes and releases an Ambu bag, breathing for him. An endotracheal tube disappears down his throat, and IVs pour fluids into both arms.

"Wheat fire." The medic himself is covered in soot and wheat chaff, his hands almost as black as Jon's. Sweat runs down his face, streaking the soot. He gives his report in a voice stretched almost to the breaking point. Whatever he saw out there, he isn't going to forget it any time soon. I make a mental note to check on him later.

"They think a combine sparked a rock. Flames took off before anyone could do a thing." The medic shakes his head. "Jon here was downwind with another farmer working on a busted truck." He wipes his head with his forearm, smearing the dirt sideways. "It's blowing a good fifty miles per hour out of the Palouse today." He shakes his head. "The other guy with Jon didn't make it. Burned to death before we got there."

"What about Jon?" I ask.

"Sorry." The medic refocuses. "Jon, forty-seven-year-old male, found down on scene, unresponsive, unconscious, oxygen saturations in the sixties, third-degree burns to at least fifty percent of his body. BP in the eighties. Two large bores, had a liter of fluid, ten of morphine, five of Versed. Second liter going in. Tough to bag."

I nod and listen to Jon's chest. His breath sounds crackly, like a wheat fire in a windstorm.

"They couldn't outrun it." The medic starts talking again. "The guys on scene said nobody could get around the fire line in time to save them."

I glance up at Jocelyn as I listen to Jon's chest.

Two blue eyes meet mine. She knows. She staggers backward as if struck, just as the hospital pastor shows up. He introduces himself and holds one of her arms. Jocelyn's boy holds the other, his face suddenly old for sixteen—a man's face.

"We'll be in the family room, waiting," the pastor says to me.

I nod.

Jocelyn staggers out of the trauma bay with her arms hooked in theirs.

I turn back to Jon. There is nothing to do for him other than pain medications. With so much of his body covered in third-degree burns, I know he will not survive no matter what is done. It won't be long now. I call airlift and the burn center across the state, three hundred miles away. I still have to try. The doc on the other end listens without a word to my presentation.

"Let us know if he's not coming" is all he says. He knows, too.

"Will do." I hang up.

I give Jon fluids and pain meds and try to keep him alive.

I sit down with Jocelyn.

"I'm Dr. Green," I introduce myself as I sit down. "One of the emergency room physicians."

She nods and clasps hands with her son.

"How bad is it?" she asks, already knowing the answer.

"Very bad."

Neither of us speak. Her son begins to sob. She straightens her back.

"Can we see him again?"

"Absolutely." I pause for a moment and take a deep breath, keeping my voice steady. "This is the time to say good-bye."

Jocelyn flinches but nods. She stands up. Her son finally breaks and collapses forward onto the floor, sobbing with his face in his hands.

"Stand up," she says to her son, her voice solid and strong.

He shakes his head.

"Stand up, David. Stand up like your father would." Her voice trembles as she loses control. "For the love of God, for the love of your father, stand up and be a man."

David stands, tears streaming down his face.

"We'll go in now," she says. "We want to say good-bye."

I stand and walk to the door, holding it open. "I'm sorry." There is nothing else to say.

I turn around, and they are gone. I stand, staring at the empty family room, the quiet ticking of the wall clock the only sound.

The seconds pass.

I shut the door.

Twenty-two years pass.

The emergency department is full. There are beds packed in the hallways with patients on them because every room is filled. The emergency department is overflowing.

A child sits on a gurney across from me, swinging his legs. An old man lies on another, sleeping, as gold-colored antibiotics drip down an IV line into his arm. A woman has a coughing fit at the end of the hall and sits down.

I walk past them all to the doctor's station, my eyes scanning the hall for Jocelyn.

There she is.

Jocelyn sits cross-legged on a gurney, reading a book and looking bored. She's in her late sixties now. There are creases and sunspots on her face. Red curls mixed with gray spill off her head, and as I get close, she blows a wayward curl out of her face with a puff.

"I'm Dr. Green, one of the emergency room physicians," I say.

She puts down her book and stares at me for a long moment, and I can see her trying to remember if it was me that day so long ago. I say nothing—it is not my place to remind her.

"I'm Jocelyn. Jocelyn Sky Gains." She extends a hand, and we shake. Meeting again.

"What brings you to the emergency department today?" I ask.

She flips her head, flicking a red curl out of her face. "I have a bladder infection." She frowns, annoyed. "I'm sorry to come to the emergency room, but urgent care is closed on Christmas Eve."

I notice the Happy Holidays sign over the nurse's station. An ambulance pulls up in the bay, and I see snow falling in its headlights.

"Have you had one before?" I ask.

"More than I can count."

I check the computer at the bedside for the results of her urine sample while she watches. Her urine is positive for nitrates, a by-product of bacteria. She's right; she has a bladder infection. I write her a prescription for antibiotics and tear off the sheet, handing it to her.

"Merry Christmas," I say.

She laughs. "Some Christmas."

She swings her legs down and stands slowly.

"Well," she says, "see you around."

She leaves again. I stand in a packed emergency department full of strangers, another Christmas Eve away from my family.

I wonder when I will see her again.

It's not long.

The operator's voice overhead interrupts my thoughts. "Code blue, room three twenty four east. Code blue, room three twenty four east."

I run into the trauma room and grab my airway equipment. It's stored in a big red toolbox so it's always ready to go anywhere in the hospital. Part of being an emergency-department doctor in a small rural hospital is that you frequently have to respond to codes elsewhere in the hospital.

A nurse I have never met jogs up the stairs to three east with me. It's a rehab wing—half nursing home, half long-term care facility. It's a place where I'm often called to codes.

We step out of the stairwell and look for the crowd. Sure enough, there are other nurses, techs, and administrators flowing toward the code.

I jog after them and step into the room.

It's Jocelyn. If it weren't for the patches of red hair on an otherwise bald scalp, I'm not sure I would recognize her. She has shrunken away like a dried-up leaf. She must be in her nineties.

She lies in the bed, curled on her side, breathing as fast as she can. Even though the room is packed with people, Jocelyn's eyes are closed, her face almost peaceful.

Standing by the window is her son. He's in his sixties now and has two grown daughters of his own. One has red hair with curls.

"What's the story?" I ask the floor nurse who called the code. She looks about nineteen. This is technically not a code blue. Yes, Jocelyn is critical, but to page a code blue overhead usually means CPR in progress. Jocelyn is not there. Not yet.

"I came in on rounds and found her like this."

I step over to Jocelyn's son.

"I'm Dr. Green, one of the emergency room physicians."

He shakes my hand, his grip firm and strong.

"Is this your mom?" I ask, knowing the answer.

He nods. "She's been sick a long time."

"Would she want to be put on a breathing machine if it's the only way to keep her alive?"

"No." He shakes his head. "But you should probably ask her yourself."

I push back through the crowd. Staff members are standing back, waiting for the decision. I squat down next to Jocelyn.

"Jocelyn, I'm Dr. Green. You are very sick. If we don't put you on a breathing machine in the next few minutes, you are going to die. Do you understand?"

Her eyes open—the same blue eyes I remember from ninety-plus years ago, when she fit in the crook of my arm.

Everything else has changed.

"Do you want me to put you on a breathing machine?" I ask.

She is breathing so fast she can hardly speak.

"I remember you," she says. Her eyes shine bright for just a second.

She pants for a moment more, catching her breath before speaking again. "Is David here?"

"We're right here, Mom." David steps forward. "The girls, too."

Jocelyn's face relaxes, and she closes her eyes.

"All right, then," she pants. "No machine."

———

Before I could speak, I was back standing in the river.

The kokanee salmon bucked from my hand. It flew into the air and landed in the river with a splash. The current swept it away before I could react.

It was gone.

I stared at the spot where it had disappeared. The current churned, never ending, never changing, never stopping.

As I stood, other fish slowly worked their way past my legs, taking their turns swimming upstream. They were nearing the end of their own journeys, their own lives, their own stories.

I stood perfectly still in the river, like a human drift net, and dreamed of catching other Jocelyns, other stories as they swam past.

John Doe

He was a John Doe.

An unknown patient.

That morning, the first and last morning I ever saw him, started for him at the Starbucks on Second and Main.

I like to imagine him pulling open the door, pausing for a moment, and then stamping the snow from his boots onto the concrete sidewalk. Maybe he tapped the side of each boot against the steel frame of the door, maybe twice each, before taking a deep breath, standing tall, and walking in like he belonged.

I can see it in my mind.

The man took his place in line with the other customers. The air of Starbucks smelled of mocha and warming cinnamon rolls. To someone who had not eaten a square meal in three days, it was akin to torture. His stomach growled, and he swallowed hard, trying not to stare at the glass cases full of glazed donuts, perfectly flaked golden brown croissants, and breakfast sandwiches.

He pulled off his wool cap and held it in his hands. It was 6:14 a.m. on a Monday, and at the moment, Starbucks was the busiest place in town. The man stood quietly in line, listening as the customers ahead of him called out order after order.

"Double cappuccino, whole milk, sugar. Dry."

"Two bacon cheddar egg sandwiches, two grande drip coffees, and…and this roll, right here." A finger with a ring on it tapped the glass display, and a scone nearly the size of a softball disappeared and dropped with a satisfying *thunk* into a brown paper bag with a mermaid on the front.

A woman stood just in front of him in the line. She wore a form-fitting pantsuit as black as the snow outside was white. Long brown hair hung perfectly straight over narrow shoulders. He took a breath and nearly gagged, the smell of boysenberry and vanilla shampoo overpowering his nose. It was a bizarre thing to smell after months of smoky campfires and musty homeless shelters.

The man stepped back ever so slightly, breathing through his mouth, ignoring her as best he could. At first she ignored him, too, flipping mindlessly through the day's Facebook feed as she waited for her turn at the front.

But the smell of her hair made his nose run. He buried his face in his sleeve and sneezed.

"Bless you," the woman said before turning casually and glancing up from her phone. If you had filmed her face—say at sixty frames per second—and then played it back in slow motion, you would have caught the millisecond-long curl of her upper lip, the flare of her nostrils, and the slight pull back of her head—the classic expression of disgust. But one millisecond later, it would be replaced again with a blank, bored look. Her eyes would be empty and unengaging, telling the man—*don't talk to me.*

The man did not care. He just stared straight ahead, biding his time as if he, too, was just another customer anxious to order his own cup of joe. He jingled the change in his pocket—maybe consciously, maybe not—so that everyone around him would know he had some money. He wasn't a vagrant, even if he was dressed like one. At least in his mind he wasn't.

With so many customers, the line should have been moving forward at a steady pace. But it wasn't. Unfortunately for everyone, the barista included, it was her first shift at Starbucks. Normally, new staff never worked a first day alone. But her coworker was at home, still curled in a ball on the floor next to the toilet from one too many Moscow Mules at a bachelorette party last night.

Don't get me wrong. The new barista was trying. But trying wasn't good enough. Not at a Starbucks. Especially not on a Monday morning. Everything she did, she did wrong—or at least that's what it seemed like. With each mistake, she grew more flustered and rushed, making even more mistakes.

"Welcome to Starbucks, what can I get going for you?" she asked the next customer. Her voice trembled, and the red splotches on her neck spread like the plague. She scribbled down the order on a pad of paper and got to work. Two minutes later, she slid a cardboard cup holder across the counter with three drinks in it.

A well-to-do housewife in a puffy white ski coat pulled the lids off each drink and leaned slightly forward, peering into the cups. She pushed the drinks back toward the barista with disgust. "This is not what I ordered."

The barista stuttered an apology and started over again. The roar of espresso machines filled the air. Faces in the line behind the woman scowled even deeper as wrists shook and watches were checked for the tenth time in ten minutes. It was now 6:41 a.m.

Everyone who had to be at work at seven was getting nervous. But no one left, not yet. A few people texted bosses that they would be late. Others glanced back toward the window and the falling snow, trying to calculate just how fast they could drive in the storm and still make it to work on time. No one had time for this. Not on a Monday morning.

Through it all the man just stood there, staring straight ahead, eyes distant. A single drop of sweat formed on his brow, right at the hairline. He jingled the change in his pocket.

"No. I said *double* latte, skim milk, *no* sugar," the woman in front of him said, her nasal voice like a slap in the face.

The girl blushed again and dumped the perfectly good drink down the sink. More grumbles. More foot tapping. More glares.

One man in line finally reached his limit. With a dramatic sigh of disgust, he bent down and grabbed his briefcase off the ground, jerking it to his side before stomping out the door. Heads nodded in agreement. This was ridiculous.

Finally, after what seemed like forever, it was the man's turn at the counter.

"Welcome to Starbucks. Sorry about the wait. What can I get going for you?" the barista said, too fried to care that a homeless man was standing before her.

"Please call me an ambulance," the man said. "I will wait for it outside." And just like that he turned and walked out, passing the twenty customers behind him. A few looked at him curiously, wondering what he had waited in line to say to the barista. But just as quickly, they forgot about him and refocused on the line ahead.

The barista thought. There was nothing about this in the training manual. But the man had wanted an ambulance. She picked up the phone, dialed 911, and asked for an ambulance to be sent to the Starbucks, Second and Main. No, she did not know why. Yes, she was an employee. No, she could not stay on the line. She hung up on the 911 operator and forced herself to smile at the next customer, who frowned back. "Welcome to Starbucks. Sorry about the wait. What can I get for you?"

"It was like he was waiting for a taxi," the medic told me later. "He was just sitting there in the snowbank on the side of the road, flakes gathering on his head. When we pulled up, he gave a little wave and stood." The medic blushed slightly. "I thought it was going to be some ridiculous complaint. Something to get him in here out of the cold. Out of the snow."

But the medic was wrong. It wasn't a nothing. The man had stepped right in front of the parked ambulance, positioning himself to make sure that the driver had eye contact with him, and tapped his chest twice, signaling that it hurt. The medic frowned. The man frowned. The man tapped his chest again, one last time, and then fell over dead.

Now he was here with me. With us. In the emergency room. A nameless patient. A John Doe.

"Another milligram of epinephrine," I say, glancing at my watch. He has been here three minutes, plus the six-minute ambulance ride, plus the approximately five minutes it took the medics to start coding him on the snow-covered side of the street in front of Starbucks. That makes it fourteen minutes since his heart stopped.

"Hold CPR," I say. I slide my fingers under his beard and feel around on his neck for a pulse. There is none. I look at the monitor. A textbook sinus rhythm marches across the screen like a drum major leading a band. It looks exactly how it should—only there is one problem. He has no pulse.

"Pulseless electrical activity," I say out loud—to myself, to my team, to no one. PEA, or pulseless electrical activity, is when the heart has electrical activity but no muscle activity. The signal is there, calling for the ventricles and atria to contract and pump the blood, but the muscle tissue of the heart is not responding.

Beat by beat, you can see it on the monitor, the heart's pacemaker firing over and over, trying to get the heart restarted before it runs out of oxygen and dies. It's like a man desperately pulling the starter cord of a chainsaw. A tree has fallen on his leg, pinning him in place. He's trapped on a remote stretch of railroad tracks as a Burlington Northern train barrels toward him. Its whistle is blowing, its wheels sparking and skidding as steel drags against steel and brakes try desperately to stop the train. But it does no good. There is too much momentum. Five thousand tons of train never stop quickly, even for a man stuck on the tracks.

The whistle blows, and the tracks begin to vibrate as the train nears. The man doubles his effort, ripping at the starter cord of the chainsaw so hard he nearly dislocates his shoulder. Over and over. Again and again and again. He is the sinoatrial node, the pacemaker tissue where the electrical signal originates in the heart. He is begging, pleading, *"Please start; please start; oh Jesus, please start."* He pulls again. The chainsaw sputters and quits. Sputters and quits. Sputters and quits. Like a heart in PEA. Like the man's heart in front me.

"Resume CPR," I say.

The tech starts it up again, the pump-pump-pump of his arm muscles substituting for the squeeze-squeeze-squeeze of the man's failing heart. The gurney shakes with each compression of the man's chest, rattling the side rails.

"No ID, nothing," the nurse behind me says. I turn around. She shrugs. She has blue gloves on and is going through the clothes we cut off him. His pants are filthy and wet from where he lost control of his bladder and lay in the snow. They are camo pants, the old camo, the kind with the big black, green, and brown blotches. The kind of pants you pick up at Goodwill or Army Surplus when you only have eight dollars to spend on clothes.

The nurse turns the pants in her hands, and nickels and dimes and quarters spill out across the ER floor, bouncing and rolling under the bed, under the counter, a few even disappearing out into the hall and around the corner like frightened mice. The sound of change hitting linoleum fills the air. It is an odd sound juxtaposed against the quiet grunts of CPR. One quarter rolls over to me, hits the tip of my shoe, and falls flat on the floor. I ignore it.

"Hold CPR," I say again. I look at the monitor. Bam-bam-bam. His heart is still ripping at that starter cord, but it's not doing a thing.

"Resume CPR," I say. "And another round of Epi." I pause. "And a milligram of Atropine."

There are courses on CPR and how to code patients. There are algorithms, flowcharts, and entire weekend-long sessions for five hundred dollars on what drug to give and when exactly to give it during a code.

But what you realize after running a hundred codes, or maybe five hundred, is that the majority of it makes no difference. Or maybe it's all so that we can feel like we did something. Like we did everything. Don't get me wrong; I follow the cookbook. I give the drugs and doses at the exact times and the exact amounts and play along as if there is good evidence that it all makes a huge difference. It doesn't matter that there is not.

But somewhere around five hundred codes, or maybe a thousand, you suddenly realize that those who are going to live, live. And those who are going to die, die.

I look back at the man on the table.

"Hold CPR," I say. I place my index finger and middle finger on his carotid artery and wait. The seconds tick past. There is nothing, not even a flicker of a beat.

"Resume CPR," I say. "Another milligram of Epi." I look at my watch. Sixteen minutes. I look back at the monitor. The electrical heartbeat is faster now. One hundred and twenty beats a minute. The train is about to hit the man on the tracks. It is so close he can see the individual rivets on the steel around the front of the headlight.

The man pulls the cord again. The chainsaw is still ice cold. With terminal horror, it suddenly dawns on the man that the chainsaw won't start: it is out of gas. No amount of pulling the rip cord is going to start it. But he pulls one last time anyway. Because a train is coming, and you have to do something.

"Any family?" I look hopefully at the medics. "Or friends with him who can identify him?"

They look at each other and back at me, shrugging.

"And nothing? No ID, no driver's license, no credit card?" I ask the nurse.

She unbuttons the breast pocket on his flannel shirt. She flips open the pocket and pulls the edges apart, holding it open for me to see. It's empty.

I turn back to the man. His face is half covered in unwashed hair. I brush it out of the way. The pores of his skin are dirty. His cheekbones are smeared with ash from campfires and sleeping on the ground. Two bushy, wild eyebrows stick out haphazardly from the lines of his face. I pull open one of his eyelids and shine in my penlight. A pupil constricts away from the light like a hand blocking the sun. It tells me his brain is still there and still working. His pupillary reflexes prove it.

I think. His collapse was witnessed by the medics. I know our medics. They don't mess around. I know they started CPR immediately. That means he had maybe fifteen seconds, thirty at the most, without blood circulating through him. But CPR started that blood right back up. They stuck a tube in his throat and oxygenated that circulating blood. It in turn went to his brain and kept it burning bright, like a breeze blowing on a flickering campfire. He's still in there. At least as long as we keep doing CPR.

I look at his face and try to imagine who he is. It's clear he is down on his luck. I wonder for a moment what made him homeless. There is always something, some last straw. Maybe the loss of a job or a loved one. Maybe a habit of alcohol transformed into a dependency before he could get a handle on it. Or maybe it was something in his brain—the onset of schizophrenia, a severe depression too strong for meds, a bipolar disorder that spiraled out of control. Whatever it was, it imploded with such violence that it cast him out into the world, alone and adrift. The currents have carried him back and forth across the country. The currents have carried him here.

I wait for the CPR to circulate the drugs through his system. You have to pump the drugs around in order for them to work, the courses say. So pump we do.

But then I start to worry. What if the reason he is homeless is something fixable? What if he's here in town to set things right? What if he was supposed to meet somebody at Starbucks, just an hour from now? Say a daughter or a son he has not spoken to in twenty, thirty years. And he was almost there. An hour away. An hour away from an apology, from forgiveness, from a new start. A second chance. What if he came all the way here just to do this one thing and then, because he was nervous, or anxious, or excited, or all three, a coronary artery in his heart chose that moment to fail.

And now all that's standing between an unresolved life and a resolved one is me. Is us. The ER. I take a breath to steady myself. If you really think about it, it's a crazy thing to bear.

"Hold CPR," I say. Still pulseless. Still electrical activity. It's mind-boggling how badly he wants to live. How hard he is trying for that second chance.

"Resume CPR."

I turn around and grab the ultrasound machine. I want to look at his heart. To see if maybe there is some fluid around it I can drain. Sometimes—well, more like almost never—fluid can accumulate around a heart, squeezing tighter and tighter, causing the pulseless electrical activity of a code. If that's the case, he just won the lottery. I can drain it with a needle and bring him back. A pericardialcentesis, it's called. With the pressure from the fluid removed, the muscles will fire right up and get back to work like a chainsaw suddenly topped off with gas and given a new spark plug. One yank, and it will be billowing smoke and buzzing so loud you'll have to cover your ears.

I look at my watch. Eighteen minutes now. The train is a foot away.

"Hold CPR," I say, placing the ultrasound probe on his chest. I turn the dials up and down. It's a black-and-white snowstorm on the little screen. A twist of my hand, a little positioning of the probe, and suddenly I can see clearly.

The train hits.

It's too late.

I can see on the ultrasound that his heart has ruptured. The ventricle, the muscle that pumps the blood, has torn open. It's like a planet struck by a massive meteor and nearly ripped into half, its magma spilling out into space, its atmosphere gone, its core flickering and going cold, going dark.

It's rare, very rare, for the ventricle of a heart to rupture like this. But it does happen. If an untreated heart attack has left a scar in the muscle, it can leave a weakness. And at some point, that weakness can fail.

It occurs to me that maybe the scar in his heart is all that's left of the day he became homeless, twenty-some years ago. Maybe something happened, something so terrible he could not bear it. Something so awful it gave him crushing, brutal, unbearable chest pain. A heart attack. But at that moment in time, he was too devastated to care. So he just lay there, wishing he could die, but failing. Eventually his chest pain stopped, and he got up and headed back out into life. But the damage was done, and the clock had started ticking. That clock has just reached zero.

I take away the probe and turn off the ultrasound. "Resume CPR," I say. I need to process this for a moment.

"What's it show?" the tech asks, his face dripping sweat from the CPR.

There is nothing we can do. It is simply unfixable. Even in a level-one trauma center, let alone in our little ER out here in the rolling hills of wheat, myocardial rupture is a death sentence.

I look at the man. He's still pink. His brain is still getting oxygen from the CPR and the ventilator. He is as alive as you or me. But the second we stop CPR, he dies.

For some reason, it hits me. Usually when I stop a code, it is on a dead person. A body that we have flailed and whipped and pushed and tried and tried to bring back with everything we have. By then they are usually gray, mottled, and clearly dead. But not this time. This time I have to call a code on a live man. A pink man. It's a first for me, even after forty-five thousand patients.

Did you ever see that movie *Signs*, the one by M. Night Shyamalan? There's a scene in there where a woman is pinned against a tree by a truck. I think her legs were gone, but I can't remember. All I remember is that as soon as they move the truck, she will die. But she's awake against the tree. Awake and alive as long as the truck is there compressing her abdomen, her aorta. The sheriff brings the husband to the scene of the accident to say good-bye. The truck can't stay there forever.

That's what I'm thinking about right now. Our CPR is the truck, and his heart is the tree.

"Cardiac rupture," I say, explaining what it is.

"What do we do for that?" the tech asks.

That's the million-dollar question.

There is nothing we can do for his body. But maybe we can at least find out who he is. Maybe call him by his name one last time before he departs.

I search him over for any jewelry or tattoos that could help us identify him. His hands are covered in callouses. Maybe he has worked his way here from some place far away. The apology he was planning, driving him to sweep the floors of a grade school in Texas after hours. To stack boxes of paper on the nightshift in a warehouse in Tennessee. To pick potatoes out in the sun in southern Idaho, sweat hiding the occasional tear that fell from his face.

"There's nothing to do," I say. "Absolutely nothing."

The tech nods, not privy to the stories running through my head.

"Should I stop?" he asks.

I don't answer. I pick up the man's clothes and search them again. I hate calling codes on John Does. The nurse was right. They are empty. Somewhere, hidden just outside of town, there is probably a backpack stashed away. In that pack, there is an ID, or a notebook, some clue as to who he is. But that pack is not here. Maybe he didn't want to look homeless when he came into town.

I pick up a boot. The sole is worn completely through. How his feet are not frostbitten I have no idea. I turn it upside down and shake it. Nothing. I pick up the other, shaking it, too, with the same result.

I look up. The nurse and tech are watching me. But they have worked with me long enough to leave me to my idiosyncrasies. I check again, wanting to make sure we did everything we could for this John Doe. I look at my watch. Thirty minutes of CPR. I know now it has made no difference. He was a dead man the moment his heart ruptured outside of Starbucks.

I guess it is time. For a moment, I debate saying something to him. He's alive, after all. Should I tell him I'm sorry that we can't save him? Should I squat by the head of the bed and try to explain that his heart has exploded and we can't keep doing CPR forever, so we are going to stop? *If you have any last thoughts, think them now.*

I don't know. I finally elect to say nothing. I hope that was OK.

"Hold CPR," I say.

There it is. The flatline. The period at the end of the last sentence of the last paragraph of the last page of the book that is him—a book that will now remain unfinished.

We all stand for a minute, the quiet whine of the flatline the only sound.

"John Doe." I look at the clock. "Time of death seven twelve."

To this day, I don't know who he was. I never found out what he was doing in our town. For a while, the coroner and the sheriff worked at identifying him. But they got nowhere. There were no leads, no clues, no missing-person reports that matched his description. Eventually the sheriff filed him away with the other John Does and moved on.

I suspect the man was cremated, and a nondescript urn with his ashes sits somewhere on a shelf in a columbarium. Maybe there is a whole shelf just for John Does and Jane Does. Maybe even a whole room. The urns sit with each other, gathering dust, forgotten in a dark basement. No one visits. No one remembers. No one ever will because there is no way to find out who they are—who they were.

I guess that is the Curse of the Does.

One time, in the mountains I stumbled upon an old headstone half buried in the ground. It was in the backcountry, in the middle of nowhere, in a half circle of Aspens hidden in some pines. I would have missed it had I not sat down for lunch using one of the trees for a backrest.

But there it was, right in front of me. I forgot about my sandwich and sat forward on my knees, brushing red and yellow leaves off the stone. I pulled up clumps of moss and weeds and swept half an inch of dirt away with my hands.

July 14, 1803. The name above it was too faded to read, only a couple of letters barely visible. But I knew who was buried there. I sat back against the tree and picked up my sandwich, chewing slowly as I shared the moment with one of the Does.

It occurred to me that day that there is a Tomb of the Unknown Soldier. A place for those who died in war but whose names were never known. A place to honor them and remember them, even though they had died anonymously.

But there is no Tomb of the Unknown Patient. No tomb for the John Does, the Jane Does, who are buried the world over. No eternal flame burns bright in their memory or honor guard that stands near. They died anonymous and forgotten.

And yet, more are added every day. In emergency rooms, in hospital rooms, sometimes in the back of ambulances as they race through the city streets with lights flashing.

Maybe it doesn't matter. Maybe we came from dust and we will return to dust, and all this is folly.

But I don't think so.

So I assigned them a monument.

It's not famous. In fact, it's almost impossible to find.

But if you are ever wandering around up in the mountains in a remote southeastern corner of Washington State, and you find a little grove of aspens surrounding a half-buried headstone, take a moment to brush it off for me. If you are so inclined, maybe stand there for a moment of silence with your hat in your hand.

Say a prayer for those men, women, and children who died anonymously and alone, anywhere in the world. Say a prayer that they might eventually find their way there, to the half-buried headstone in the woods. And once there, that they might find each other and thus find comfort in company. Comfort in the fact that, though anonymous, they are not forgotten.

Take a moment to remember them, there at the Tomb of the Unknown Patient.

Holster

I once met a man who tried to kill himself.

He denied it when I asked him.

It was the middle of the night. He had been driving an empty stretch of road south of town known as The Gutter. It was a two-and-a-half-mile stretch of pavement that wound its way through the mountains like a snake slithering back and forth between half-buried stones.

In some remote canyon, at some crucial moment, some last wall of resistance inside of him crumbled. When he could no longer resist, he yanked his steering wheel to the left, swerving his car across the double line and smashing through the barrier. In an instant, his car was airborne, tumbling like a poorly punted football before landing with a splash in the river below.

If it weren't for some college kids camping along the shore, his story would be over. He would be dead. But instead, he was here, in the ER with me at four fifteen in the morning, wrapped in a frazzled wool blanket left behind by the medics. His hair was still wet and dripping, his lips still blue, his teeth still chattering.

I checked him over. He was not injured, just cold.

"What happened?" I asked.

He stared down at his hands, slowly opening and closing his fingers, avoiding my gaze. "Don't know," he said, his voice quiet.

He was in his early forties, with thin black hair on a pale scalp. Even sitting, he stooped like a man twice his age, his back bent like a hunter's bow, the string pulled back much too far and about to snap. As I waited, a chill passed through him. He shook violently, his entire frame quaking from the mix of cold and fading adrenaline.

Something about the way he spoke shook me. It was clear I was in the presence of some absolute, some complete, some final and terminal sadness. It extended out from him like a sponge that drained the light and hope from the walls of the ER room. It made it hard to breathe.

I took a step back.

"Was there anyone else in the car with you?"

He shook his head and looked up at me. "It's just me now."

I tried for several minutes to get more out of him. He denied that he was trying to hurt himself, but words only mean so much. I could see the truth in his face.

A few minutes later, I sat out at the desk, looking through his past medical records on the computer. I found two other odd accidents in the last three months.

First, his ex-wife had stopped by one day and found him passed out in the garage, an empty whiskey bottle in his hand and the car still running. A few minutes more and he wouldn't have lived. That time he insisted he had been sitting in the car listening to music and fallen asleep, unaware that the car was still running. He was brought to the ER and evaluated by a colleague of mine. He had been detained for a suicide attempt and sent to a psychiatric facility for a couple of days. A week later, he was discharged on an antidepressant.

Three weeks after that, he had crashed his wife's car, crossing the highway's center line to hit a semi head-on. By some miracle, he had survived again. That time, according to records, he claimed to have swerved in order to avoid a deer. Once again, he was evaluated and let go. The rest of his medical history was pretty standard stuff high blood pressure, a couple of visits for some mild asthma, a visit for chest pain. Nothing really.

I logged out and stood up. I grabbed a warm blanket from the warmer for him.

"How are you doing?" I asked.

The man lay on the bed, his eyes closed. "Fine."

I sat down next to him. "You've had some bad accidents the last couple of months."

He just lay there, ignoring me.

"Any chance this wasn't an accident?" I asked as gently as I could.

"Nope."

I sat there for a minute more in silence. He wasn't going to talk. I couldn't make him. I stood up slowly and left.

I went back to the computer and searched a little further back in his history. And then I found it. One year ago to the day, his doctor had called in a prescription for Xanax. The chart note said it was for an acute grief reaction. I read further. The man's young son had died. My patient had accidentally backed over his toddler in the driveway, killing him on the spot.

Since then there were multiple prescriptions for depression, for anxiety, for insomnia. And then, three months ago, the accidents had started.

I called our mental-health worker and explained the case.

"I can't detain him," she told me an hour later after evaluating him. "He denies any suicidal thoughts. He swears it was an accident."

"Did you ask about his son?" I asked.

"I did." She folded her arms across her chest. "He acknowledges his grief. He admits that it has been rough. Apparently, his own father blames him for the death of his little boy. But when I try to get him to connect it to the accidents, he clams up. He has an excuse for every single one about why he wasn't trying to hurt himself."

"And you believe him?" I ask.

"Not in the least," she said. "But I can't legally detain someone based on a suspicion."

I leaned back in my chair. "You know as well as I do that he's going to succeed one of these times."

She took a deep breath. "I know. I agree with you. I wish there was something I could do." She looked away from me. "He killed his own son," she said quietly. "Can you even begin to imagine how horrible that would be? I'm not sure even if he admitted it that anything we do or say would stop him in the long run."

It has been five years, maybe more, since that night in the ER. I never saw the man again. I have never looked up his record or even opened his chart. I am afraid to find out what happened to him.

For the longest time, I couldn't get him out of my head. The same questions kept haunting me: What would it take to stop a man like him, one who had completely committed himself to ending his own life? Was there anything that could overcome a grief like his—one so awful, so all-consuming that it blotted out the very sky?

I kept coming up with nothing.

Grief like that was just too much.

And then, one night, I found myself alone, driving the same stretch of road through the mountains. The sun was setting on the canyon walls, coloring them a deep red. There were no other cars around. I slowed down and took my time, following the double yellow line on the pavement as it wound its way back and forth next to the river. And just like that, the memory of the man joined me. I could feel a story born from his grief start to take hold in my thoughts.

At first it was nothing more than a vague feeling, a few scattering lines and letters tumbling about. I drove on, waiting. And then, ever so slowly, the lines of a face formed. A tired face, a dark face, a man's face. And suddenly I knew this man in my head, this man in this story, had killed his son in an accident, not unlike my patient.

And this was his story.

For some, grief is an illness.

An influenza that you contract out of catastrophe. One day you take a breath, and there it is, already inside of you, spreading from cell to cell faster than you can respond.

It hits you hard and fast. Suddenly, nothing else matters. Your limbs grow heavy, your thoughts drag and stagger, and your mind stumbles about like a rabid animal fixated on the loss that started it all—*what if, what if, what if.*

The first few days are the worst. Even breathing takes effort. You try and go through the motions of life, but you fail. Family and friends rush to your side to lend support; even strangers hold the door for you when they see your face. You don't argue. You need all the help you can get, and you know it.

But then something you didn't think possible happens. Life goes on. The sun comes up, the sun goes down, the sun comes up. Your soul rallies and responds to the infection. Some part of you begins to develop immunity, or at least resistance. More time passes, and though you are sad, you find that your grief is compartmentalized and contained. It's now like a tumor walled off in a muscle. On bad days, it still hurts—you feel it when you hike or run, but most of the time you barely notice it at all. You are just too busy.

But for a select few, an unlucky few, grief is different. It is a powder instead of a sickness, an insidious dust that finds its way into every fold and joint of your life. It gets in your mouth and darkens your teeth. It even cracks your lips. When you eat your favorite food, it coats your tongue. All you taste is dirt.

For some reason, your eyes seem to collect it. When you look at a loved one, your vision is dark. Your eyes burn and sting as if you are standing in a smoke-filled room. You try to blink it away, but that only makes it worse. The grains of dust, of grief, are just too fine. All you can do is look away from those you love with eyes squeezed shut, your jaw clenched, and tears running down your face.

The very worst part is that it does not kill you. It keeps you alive. And it uses every second of every minute of every day to grind your loss into you over and over until finally you, too, break apart into powder, into dust.

When that moment comes, and you realize that you are not going to get better, no matter how much time passes, you have to make a choice: find a way to live with the pain or do something final to put an end to it once and for all.

For those who decide to end it, to end their lives in order to stop the pain, it takes something akin to an act of God to stop them.

But sometimes, just sometimes, when God is not looking, someone else may step in. It may even be a child.

———

Jeremiah Kindred was walking in a field of wheat when he decided he was going to kill himself. It was August, and the wheat was ready for harvest. It stood waist high, the top grains so heavy that the slightest breeze tipped the fields into motion. Gusts darkened the face of the hills as the wheat waved and shook, changing shades. The surface of the earth around him looked more like the glowing embers of a fire pit than the grains that feed the world.

Jeremiah walked with his hands out, dragging his palms through the wheat. At the top of each kernel of wheat rise several long, thin whiskers called the brush. And like the threads of a brush, they tickle the hand as they paint the palm. Since he was a boy, Jeremiah had touched thousands, maybe even millions, of brushes. It had always brought him a quiet pleasure, like the solidness of oak or the cool touch of a shaded stone on a hot day.

This time it didn't. It brought him nothing. It just scraped across his palms as he walked. He closed his hands and slid them into his pockets. It was at that moment that he realized he was done. He would not, he could not, go on.

It didn't matter that his fields would remain uncut. It didn't matter that his wife and daughter were at home waiting for him. It didn't matter that nothing he did would return his son to the world.

He was blinded by the dust.

Blinded by grief.

There it is, Jeremiah whispered to himself. He could feel the decision swing shut and lock behind him, trapping him on a path with only one possible outcome. The thought of suicide did not frighten him or even surprise him. Some part of him had known since the funeral that this day would eventually arrive. He had fought it for all he was worth, but he had lost. And now he knew it.

Jeremiah took one last look at his fields. It would have been a good harvest. A gust, stronger than the rest, shoved him back with a blast and he stepped away, off balance. He tucked his chin to his chest, squinting his eyes, and turned so the wind was at his back. With his hands in his pockets, he half walked, half jogged the straight line back to his truck.

He climbed into the old Ford and turned the key. *Even my eyes hurt*, he thought to himself. He blinked away tears, shifted into first, and was gone.

Once on the road, he did not rush. He drove slowly and deliberately, taking his time down the empty two-lane road as it wound and climbed through the rolling fields like an unspooling thread. He could feel the force of the decision gathering momentum and pushing him along, carrying him forward as the current of a river shoves a log downstream toward a waterfall.

It was odd to think that the end was finally here. Jeremiah studied it in his mind. He picked it up and turned it over and over, feeling for cracks, for weakness, for some sign that he could break it apart. The decision seemed to be a blend of relief, of fear, of sadness, and even of anger. Jeremiah squeezed it tight with his mind, like a stone in the hand, and he found it to be immutable and uncompressible. Today really was the end.

Most of us spend the last hours of our lives remembering other people. We think about the moments we shared or the moments we lost—perhaps that one trip to the lake with the grandkids or the first time we held a daughter or son.

But Jeremiah did not think of these things. He looked ahead.

The Blue Mountains of Eastern Oregon filled the horizon, their slow rise and smooth shape across the arch of the sky giving them the illusion of proximity. After a lifetime in the valley, it still surprised Jeremiah that something that looked so close could be so far away.

For forty-six years, he had hiked and hunted them. The peaks and valleys held Jeremiah's memories the same way they held canyons and pines. Driving toward them, he felt himself driving into the past and the end of his future at the same time.

A half an hour later, the road narrowed and turned to gravel before beginning to climb. Jeremiah slowed as the truck began the long ascent into the mountains. His Ford bounced back and forth in the knee-deep ruts of Forest Service Road 181, the inside rattling and shaking so hard he had to brace himself with a hand on the ceiling.

Behind the truck, with each bounce and skid, plumes of fine silt burst from the road and tumbled after the pickup, burying the tire tracks as quickly as they formed.

But Jeremiah ignored what was behind him. Up ahead now was all that mattered. Toward the peaks. Toward the sky. Toward the end. If he had to do it, this was the place. Here, where he had honeymooned with his wife twenty-three years ago. Here, where he had learned to hunt with his father. Here, where his only son had died.

The memories of those we love are a funny thing—a blessing and a curse, a two-edged sword. One side of the blade protects us, warding off fear, loneliness, and doubt with the memory of a child's smile or a spouse's touch.

But the other side of the same blade cuts us. The memories that we feel so deeply also cause us pain. They remind us that we are separate from those we love. And that separation carves out a space within us that can only be filled with the return presence of another.

But when a person dies, that moment cannot arrive. Those spaces stay empty. Yet the memories do not stop. They keep carving away at us, like a miner who can't stop digging deeper into the earth. Soon, if one does not make peace with the loss, the memory will carve too deeply into the person who carries it, until the whole mine collapses down around them.

The road dipped, taking a slight detour over a washed-out berm around a corner. Jeremiah braked, shifting into four-wheel drive, and started again. The sun rounded some trees and shone in his eyes. He flipped down the visor. It was almost noon.

"By nightfall," he said out loud, half startling himself, "I will be gone."

He nodded, as if in agreement with himself. He knew now both where and when he would do it. He clenched his jaw and accelerated again, the truck shaking violently.

Why did he bring his son to these mountains in the first place? His eyes filled with tears.

Jeremiah tried to understand.

He drove on.

And then the first memory came to him. It cut him ever so slightly but then, just as quickly, consoled him. His father had left him alone in the woods for the first time just a few miles from where he was now.

Jeremiah remembered.

———

It was September. He was long and lanky and ten years old. The middle of the night. A nameless ridge among thousands of nameless ridges above the headwaters of the Wenaha River in eastern Oregon.

"Don't come look for me," his father whispered, his voice firm as he squatted down in front of Jeremiah. "I'll be back at dawn."

Before Jeremiah could protest, his father stood and left, making his way down the ridgeline into the night. Jeremiah stayed put, too stunned to move or call out. This was not part of the plan.

Jeremiah watched him go. This was supposed to be a hunting trip. Together.

A tightness rose in his chest and coiled round his lungs, cinching snug. Jeremiah fought to breathe as he watched his father's outline disappear over the far edge of the ridge, swallowed by the night sky like a stone dropped in a bucket of oil.

Jeremiah tilted his head to the side and strained to listen, but all he could hear was his heart pounding in his chest.

He was alone.

Alone.

It was a new sensation for a ten-year-old boy. He had been alone before, in his room or walking home from school, but that was different. That was like sitting on a horse still tied to a post and calling it riding. This was alone with a capital *A*, the horse tearing through the woods, wide-eyed with panic, snapping branches and jumping logs at a mad gallop with Jeremiah clinging to its back in terror.

He tried to think. For a moment, he considered running after his father and calling out for him. But some part of Jeremiah knew he would not find him. Not until dawn. Not until whatever was supposed to happen had happened. His father was gone, and this was a test. It could be no clearer.

Jeremiah inhaled and squeezed his rifle tight, pulling it to his chest. Even at ten years old, he knew enough to know that predators hunted these same ridgelines, predators that could just as easily kill a lone boy as disembowel a horse.

He sat in the dark, a mile down in an ocean of fear, afraid to move, afraid to blink.

A stick snapped nearby, and he forgot all about his father. *Go away*, he mouthed, *please go away*. Images of bears, of mountain lions, of a darkness vague and shifting and inching nearer filled his mind. He felt his self-control weaken and stretch thin. *Run-run-run*—the words repeated themselves inside him.

But something else was taking hold inside of Jeremiah as well. It had started slowly, almost imperceptibly, like the first light of day. With each moment, it grew, trickling in and working its way against gravity up his spine. It pooled between his shoulder blades and ran out his arms and legs. He sat straighter and opened his eyes.

Run-run-run, his mind still said.

"No." Jeremiah spoke it aloud. "No, I will not."

He refused to move, terrified and thrilled at the same time.

At the sound of his voice, whatever was near crashed off through the branches and into the night. It did not return.

Jeremiah sat, watching the moon float up into the sky, its off-white color spilling out over the trees, the canyons, and the mountains. He thought about his father. He did not understand. Why would you leave your son alone in the mountains? Maybe he did not know his father after all.

An hour passed.

As the night wore on, Jeremiah began to forget about himself, about being alone, about his father, even about being a boy. His hands stopped shaking, and his breathing slowed. A movement on a distant ridge caught his eye. He set down the rifle, making sure it was within arm's reach, and dug through his pack for the binoculars.

Back and forth, up and down, side to side, he glassed the ridges in a smooth, never-ending motion. He let his eyes walk the lines, climb the stones, poke and prod through every bush, every tree, every dip and valley. He breathed deeply, steadying his hands, steadying the lenses, and steadying himself. The cold night air filled his lungs, and the memory of the moment formed inside him.

A small stone broke loose somewhere close and tumbled down the draw. Jeremiah turned and stared toward the sound through the binoculars. All he could see was a rocky ledge, perhaps a hundred feet away, the twinkling stars visible just beyond.

The rock did not change, but the skyline behind it did. A massive bull elk rose into view, stepping and stopping, stepping and stopping, cresting the ridge. It was like watching the bull push its way out of the earth and into the world one stone at a time. It stopped at the top, its bulk black against the moonlit sky, just fifty feet away. It turned its head ever so slightly, and Jeremiah sucked in his breath. Huge antlers, wider than his father was tall, sat atop its head.

For a moment, neither moved. Jeremiah knew that the bull, too, was walking its eyes and ears through the lines, the stones, the brush. It, too, was checking for danger, checking for threats. A guttural grunt broke the silence, and the bull shook its head and started forward.

Jeremiah lay spellbound, forgetting about his gun. Behind the bull they came. One by one, the rest of the herd broke the ridgeline, following the bull. They came closer, their hooves crunching quietly on the dry grass. Jeremiah could just hear the whistle of their breath as they neared, a sound unlike any other in the world.

The big bull passed first, walking just inches from where Jeremiah lay sprawled on the rock, half hidden by a bush. Its side was so huge it reminded Jeremiah of a freight train, slowly rolling past the brush. Without thinking, he reached out his hand through the branches and dragged his fingertips through the hide of the bull as it passed. It was wet with dew. Next came a small female followed closely by a limping calf. He let his fingers run along their sides as well. Others followed. One by one he touched them all, and they touched him.

The bull, down the trail behind him now, bugled out over the canyon. Another bull, somewhere on a distant ridge, bugled back. And then, just like that, they were gone. Jeremiah was alone again. But this alone was different. This alone belonged to Jeremiah.

Minutes later, hours later, the horizon turned gray with the first light.

Dawn came.

Jeremiah spotted his father working his way back up the ridge. He watched him come. When he crested the top, Jeremiah stood up and gave a loud whoop. His father, seeing Jeremiah standing atop the rock with the sky behind him and the rifle raised over his head in victory, gave a joyous shout back.

"Someday I will bring my son to these mountains," Jeremiah said when the two were face-to-face.

His father stopped cold in his tracks, as if he had been struck. He started to speak but had to stop himself. He looked away.

A crow flying overhead called out, its cries echoing up the canyons.

Jeremiah stood tall before his father. For the first time in his life, Jeremiah felt the rightness of the world.

———

The dirt road leveled out as Jeremiah's truck neared the top of Squaw Ridge. The sun moved further west in the sky. The narrow gravel ballooned out into a half-circle turnaround before ending altogether at a wall of pines.

He drove to the foot of the trees and shut off the engine. A cloud of dust engulfed the truck. Sweat ran down and pooled in the small of his back against the vinyl of the seat. He ignored it. That night had been over thirty years ago now. The memory almost seemed to belong to someone else.

He closed his eyes and rested his head against the seat. That night, the night of the elk, life had felt like such a gift, like a rich tapestry woven out into the world from these mountains. All he had to do was take a step in any direction and there it was, shining bright and waiting for him. But not now. And not ever again.

What he wouldn't give to sit down with his father one last time and ask for advice, for help. His father would know what to do. He always did. But his father was gone, same as his son.

That left just Jeremiah. "It's just me now," he whispered to the empty cab. He watched as dust gathered into little clumps and tumbled down the windshield in front of him. One by one they fell, leaving long thin tails made of sunlight where the dust had been.

He wiped his brow. Was this the right thing to do? Was killing yourself an act of bravery or cowardice? Would his father have done the same if he were in this position? A fresh wave of grief and shame crashed into Jeremiah, knocking him back in the seat. His eyes grew distant and wide. He didn't fight it. He never did anymore. He just let it tear into and feed upon every part of him.

He looked over at the daypack on the seat beside him, afraid of what lay inside. The air of the cab suddenly felt unbearably stale. He gasped, clutching his chest. This had to stop. With his shoulder, he pushed open the door and fell out of the truck, collapsing to his knees in the dirt.

He stayed on all fours for a moment, trying to slow his breathing, letting the panic pass as he had learned to do. The smell of diesel exhaust mixed with the scent of the high-country tamaracks. It calmed him. This place, these trees, these mountains—if the answer was anywhere, it was here.

He stood and grabbed the daypack off the passenger seat. He reached into the bag, felt around for a moment, and pulled out the reason he had come. He stepped back from the door and set it on the hood, staring.

His father's .44 Smith and Wesson revolver shone in the bright sunlight like a mirror.

Jeremiah took a deep breath and picked it up.

His father had killed a man with this gun.

———

Jeremiah was fourteen.

It was the end of the season, the time of year when snow capped the peaks but still spared the canyons below. The hour was late, and the light was low. It was day five of what was supposed to be a three-day hunt. But the massive tracks they had stumbled across on day two were too big to ignore.

Together, he and his father had tracked the elk over ridgelines, through scree fields, across rivers. Somehow, it always seemed to stay just a step ahead, just out of range, just out of sight. But they were close now, the closest they had been the entire hunt.

Jeremiah and his father waded through the river into the canyon right before dark. The water was fast flowing and dangerous, churning white even in the low light. Halfway across, Jeremiah stepped on a loose stone and fell, the river's grip instantly tearing him from his feet. He would have gone down with his pack and rifle still strapped to his back had his father not grabbed him and dragged him back to his feet. Without a word, they continued on.

They found him on the far side. The bull was feeding in a small field, ripping up clumps of grass and roots, deafened to their approach by the roar of the rapids. Jeremiah and his father stalked close and stopped. It was late, almost dark. If they shot him now, they would have to spend the night cleaning him.

After a brief discussion, they decided to wait. They would take him at dawn. In the meantime, there was nowhere for the bull to go. The canyon narrowed to a dead end at the falls a quarter mile upstream. Jeremiah and his father backtracked silently, crossing over the river again, and set up camp in their own small clearing. If the bull elk tried to leave the canyon, he would have to pass them.

Jeremiah started the fire while his father hiked down to the river's edge to chop wood. The air was damp and thick and wrapped around Jeremiah's limbs like wet cloth, making every movement heavy and slow. He shivered, scooting closer to the fire. It was going to be a brutally cold night. The temperature fell even further, and

Jeremiah watched as the mountaintops above the valley disappeared in a wall of white.

Sure enough, an hour later, big wet flakes mixed with rain fell from the sky. Wet snow began to gather into small patches on the ground. It lined the crevices of logs, the folds of clothes, and the bare patches scattered between the trees. Soon the entire world turned white.

Jeremiah sat on a stump by the campfire, cooking dinner. A small pot of stew rested in the ashes just inside the fire ring. He lifted the lid and stirred it with the blade of his pocketknife, and the smell of cooking meat, potatoes, and carrots filled the air. His stomach growled, and his mouth watered. If his father didn't hurry up, there wouldn't be any left.

The stew began to boil. He grabbed a stick and hooked the little pot, pulling it back from the flames just enough to keep it from burning. His stomach growled louder, and he stirred the stew again. Only this time something felt wrong. That sense of peace he had felt just a moment before had disappeared as quickly as the wet flakes falling into the fire. In its place was a vague sense of something... something not right. The sound of his father's axe stopped. The hair on the back of Jeremiah's neck began to rise. Someone was watching him.

He looked instinctively to the far side of the clearing, the edge of the firelight, and his heart stopped. A man stood, stooped and hidden in the woods, eyes locked on Jeremiah.

A minute passed.

Neither moved.

Finally, the man took a few steps into the clearing. He moved slowly, slinking along like a stray mongrel drawn by the smell of blood. He stopped again and stared at Jeremiah.

Neither spoke.

A gust of wind hit the fire. It popped and cracked in protest, smoking heavily, nearly going out. Jeremiah threw another log into the flames. When he looked up, the man was closer, maybe thirty feet away.

Jeremiah studied him in the light of the fire, trying to stay calm.

Gray-streaked hair lay matted against the stranger's oversized head. A huge beard, caked with dirt, covered the man's chest. Two dark eyes sat back in a cachectic face, darting between Jeremiah, the fire, and the woods behind him. The man slid a hand inside a tattered flannel jacket and removed a silver flask, taking a long swig. He wiped his mouth with the back of his sleeve and smiled, revealing a mouth full of rotten teeth.

But it was the man's rifle that Jeremiah could not stop staring at. It was an old lever-action .30-.06 slung over the man's left shoulder. Instead of a leather strap, frayed twine held it in place. The barrel was as dirty as the man was. Even in the low light, Jeremiah could tell the steel was dented and rusted. The rifle pointed straight up, directly toward the heavy clouds overhead. Rain and snow fell into the barrel, but the man did not seem to care.

He took another swig from the flask.

He spoke.

"You here alone?"

Jeremiah didn't answer.

"I *said*," the man slurred, "you here alone?"

Jeremiah shook his head no.

The man started to speak and then stopped, startled by something. Jeremiah looked back to the tent behind him. His father stood there, axe in hand, silently taking it all in.

The man stepped closer to the fire, closer to Jeremiah.

Jeremiah's father moved slowly and deliberately, like a wolf before a coyote, his lack of speed more threatening than the axe in his hand. He stepped between Jeremiah and the man.

The man stepped back.

Jeremiah leaned to the side to see around his father.

The man took another swig from his flask and held it out toward them.

When his father did not move, the man spit on the ground through the slit between his two front teeth, putting the flask back inside his coat. He took another step forward.

Jeremiah's father turned and threw the axe from his hand. It spun end over end and buried itself an inch deep in a fallen cedar at the edge of camp. No words could speak more clearly. The stranger was not welcome here.

The man laughed and spit on the ground again.

He began to speak. He said he was a hunter like they were. He said he had hunted these hills a long time, like they had. He said all hunters were brothers in camp.

His father still did not speak, did not move, did not react at all. He just stood perfectly still as rain collected and ran from the back brim of his oilskin hat. Jeremiah could not see his face, but he knew it was calm, steady, and in control. Such was his father.

The man's voice grew louder. He spoke faster. More spittle flew. Threats came, vague at first, then direct. But he did not come closer.

"Hunters share their food with other hunters in the backcountry," he said. "No one should go hungry when there is enough for everyone."

He wiped his nose and looked around the camp. He was about to speak again when he spotted the rifle that belonged to Jeremiah's father. He couldn't help himself. He stared, avarice igniting both eyes.

The custom .30-.06 sat leaned up against the tent, under the fly. Even in the low light of the fire, it glowed like a gem. The barrel glistened with a fresh sheen of oil, so perfect it reflected the jumping flames of the campfire like a mirror. As the man watched, a single drop of condensation beaded at the top of the barrel and slid down harmlessly, unable to touch the steel underneath.

The stock of the rifle was dark oak and worn smooth from use. Its side was fine, dark, and precise. A leather strap, handcrafted by his father specifically for the rifle, twisted slowly back and forth from the top of the barrel. It was the gun of a master hunter.

The stranger licked his lips, still staring at the rifle. He seemed to have forgotten about the food. Jeremiah could feel something coming, something dark and dangerous. He grew afraid.

The man pulled out his flask once more and took a long drink, tipping it upside down to show it was gone before tossing it aside.

"I am joining you for dinner."

He took a step closer.

Jeremiah's father unbuttoned the front of his slicker and pulled it back, resting his hand on the .44 that never left his hip in the mountains, the .44 that was as much a part of his father as his own bones and blood.

The man's smile faded. He said, "It's not right to keep a man hungry when you have more than enough. It's not right to turn a man away from a hot fire on a cold night. It's not right for you to have and others to not. I'm a hunter, too, goddamn it. I'm a hunter, too."

The man pointed at Jeremiah. "If there's not enough, the boy can go hungry. It's good for a boy to sleep in the mountains with an empty stomach. It teaches him to be a man."

He coughed a deep, wet cough.

"Give me some food."

He took another step.

"Give me some food."

Jeremiah did not breathe.

His father spoke. "No."

The word hung in the air as if nailed to the sky. It was solid, unmovable, untouchable as the mountains around the three of them.

The man spit on the ground. "Curse you. And curse your son. May death find you both before dawn."

He turned, shuffling and slinking, stumbling back toward the tree line.

A wet log in the fire popped. The man spun, unslinging his gun and aiming it at Jeremiah's father in a practiced motion, dropping to one knee as he did so. He moved impossibly fast for someone who had seemed so drunk just a moment before.

Jeremiah's father drew the revolver. Even now, his movements seemed slow and deliberate, unhurried and unafraid.

He raised his arm, took aim, and shot the man in the center of the chest.

The stranger was dead before he hit the ground.

That night, Jeremiah and his father lay in their sleeping bags, listening to the sound of the snow and rain on the tent walls. They had buried the man down by the river. A small stack of stones the only sign of what had happened that night.

"Did you have to kill him?" Jeremiah asked.

His father did not answer at first. The walls of the tent shook from the wind. Outside, trees snapped and crashed to the ground as the river roared near flood level from the storm.

"Some things can only be stopped with a bullet," his father said.

Jeremiah waited for more, but that was it.

Barely sixty seconds later, his father's snores joined the sound of the wind.

———

Some things can only be stopped with a bullet, Jeremiah whispered to himself, remembering. He understood now. He stepped back from the gun sitting on the hood of the pickup and wiped his face. He would never forget that day. Never forget his father being ready to protect his son.

Jeremiah opened the passenger side of the truck and felt around on the floor under the passenger seat, bringing out a folded sweat shirt. He opened the edges slowly and picked up what was in the middle.

A holster.

The holster.

He held it out in front him like a poisonous snake and let it dangle in the sunlight.

Last night was the first time he had touched it since Jonathan had died. It had still been in the boy's room, next to his bed, hanging from the stand where his wife had left it after the funeral.

It had taken almost an entire bottle of Jack Daniel's even to step into the boy's room. Everything was still exactly as Jonathan had left it six months ago. A glass of water sat next to the boy's bed, long since evaporated, its sides dirty from dust in the air.

Jeremiah picked up the bright-blue pillow, held it to his face, and took a breath. Jonathan's smell tore out his heart. He dropped the pillow, trembling, and braced himself against the wall to keep from collapsing. He couldn't shake the thought that the boy was trapped nearby, just out of reach, just out of touch for all eternity.

Jeremiah stared at the holster in his hands. It was oversized by modern standards, made to carry a big gun. The bright leather was worn smooth, the star that had been stamped into it at one time long since gone.

Jeremiah's father had passed it down to Jeremiah, just as his father had to him, and his father's father before that. It was the only family heirloom that seemed to matter.

Jonathan had loved the holster, and Jeremiah had given it to him for his sixth birthday. His father had not approved, but Jeremiah hadn't cared. By then, Jonathan already wore it around the house every day. Unlike its previous owners, who had always carried a gun in it, Jonathan found his own use for it.

The boy collected superheroes. Lots of them. His room was filled with box after box of figurines. Every Saturday morning, he picked out ten of his favorites. Those ten went with him wherever he went. Last fall, Jeremiah had been packing for a hunting trip with a friend. The holster had been lying on top of his duffels when Jonathan found it.

Jonathan had walked into the kitchen with the holster slung over his shoulder and across his chest like an ammo belt from a movie. In the center of his chest hung the pouch for the gun, only instead of a pistol, several lucky superheroes peeked out over the top. From then on, the holster was his. It never left his chest. At night, he hung it beside his bed so that, as he said, they could keep watch and keep him safe from the dark.

Now Jonathan was gone, but the holster was still here. Jeremiah strapped it to his waist, put the .44 in the pouch, shouldered his pack, and started hiking. He did not look back. He clenched his jaw so hard his teeth ached. He would see Jonathan soon enough. He would set things right with his son.

———

Jeremiah hiked, lost in memories. His feet crunched in the dry grass, his boots scuffed against the rocks left exposed, and his heart ached from the vast hole left in the center of his life.

He came to a small game trail and followed it without thinking. It snaked along, taking long slow undulations back and forth beneath the deep blue of a late August sky. The trail followed the ridgeline, no different from the thousand other ridgelines in the surrounding mountains, no different save for the man hiking across it in search of a spot to kill himself.

The afternoon passed. The trail faded to nothing. He kept climbing. Up and up he went, into the high country. He came to a rock formation at the top of a rise. He passed between the stones, the spires stuck up into the sky around him like broken Greek columns.

He had stopped here once with his father, too. A sudden storm had caught them on the ridgeline, and they had taken shelter from the wind among the spires. Gusts had howled through the rocks as rain blew sideways to the earth. Jeremiah had left his coat back at the tree stand, even though he was old enough to know better. He was sixteen. He had sat shivering, squatted over his rifle, trying to keep it dry. He was soaked to the bone and miserable, but he bit his tongue and stayed quiet. It was his own fault, and he knew it.

After an hour in the rain, he was so cold he could hardly stand it. And then, without a word, Jeremiah's father had taken off his own slicker and placed it over Jeremiah's shoulders. Jeremiah had tried to say no, tried to protest, but he was so cold the words would not form on his lips. For the next two hours, he watched his father shiver and pace as they waited out the storm.

Once the rain had stopped and the sun had come out, they started on their way again. Jeremiah had asked why his father had done it. Why had he given him the slicker when it was Jeremiah's own carelessness that had caused the problem in the first place?

His father looked directly at him and answered, "A man's job is to protect his son."

———

Jeremiah passed the rocks and kept going, his father's voice repeating over and over in his head.

A man's job is to protect his son.

Jeremiah said it aloud, "A man's job is to protect his son."

It was to be Jonathan's first night ever sleeping in a tent, his first night in the mountains. The boy had just turned six the week before, announcing at the celebration with a mouth full of birthday cake that all he wanted this year was to camp in the mountains like his father.

Jeremiah was delighted. He planned everything down to the smallest detail. He wanted it to be perfect, to be memorable, to be unforgettable. He wanted to plant the seeds of an unbreakable bond with the place he loved. To give to Jonathan what his father had given to him.

Jeremiah chose a place called Three Rivers for the trip. Three separate canyons, each with its own river and individual drainage, came together at the base of a mountain peak and created a tiny lake that ultimately overflowed and became the Wenaha River. At different times, different rivers dominated. A distant rainstorm to the north would create one flow. To the east another. And to the west another altogether.

Thus, some days the little lake was a blackish green, its surface smooth as ink, not a wrinkle or fold visible in the water. Hours later, the same surface could transform into a churning, frothing maelstrom of motion and mud as the rivers slammed into each other and fought for dominance.

It was a spectacular place to camp. The ever-changing surface and sounds of the water created an unforgettable companion, one Jonathan would surely remember forever.

They drove as far back into the mountains as they could, following abandoned and forgotten forest service roads. Jeremiah felt like a child at Christmas as he drove, telling Jonathan stories of his adventures in the woods. Jonathan ate it up, asking questions about everything, pointing out the trees, the deer feeding in the fields, the shape of the mountains themselves. He was as excited as his father.

They parked the truck and hiked the two miles in to Three Rivers. When they arrived, the lake was glass. Jonathan went down to play at the water's edge while Jeremiah stayed up above in the trees to set up camp.

He put up the tent, lay out their sleeping bags, and went to collect firewood. He was picking up sticks from a fallen cedar when he heard it. The roar of the canyons. The lake was waking. He returned to camp and hustled down to the water to watch the show with Jonathan.

But Jonathan was gone.

All that was left was the holster at the water's edge, spinning slowly in an eddy, a few plastic figurines floating facedown around it.

Jeremiah never saw Jonathan again.

He should have been watching.

A father's job was to protect his son.

Jeremiah touched the handle of the gun as he hiked. It scalded his skin. The sun had been on it for the last hour, and the handle had absorbed the heat. He wondered briefly just how hot steel had to be to melt.

He thought of that day again. The image of the empty holster spinning in the water had never left him. It spun in his dreams, waking him. It spun when he spoke, interrupting him. It spun every minute of every hour of every day since that moment—just out of sight, just out of reach, just like Jonathan.

It never ended.

He had slowly come to realize that there was only one way to make the holster stop spinning. A wave of nausea passed through him, and he squeezed the handle of the revolver even tighter, forcing it down into the holster. A blister formed at the base of his right ring finger where it touched the hot steel. *Let it burn*, he thought to himself, refusing to flinch or pull away.

His left hand slid into his pants pocket. He picked up the single bullet he had been saving. It was cool to the touch. Habit took over, and he began rolling it back and forth between his fingers as he hiked. The bullet was his touchstone, the key to stopping the spinning, to putting an end to the day that had no end.

Hours passed, and still he climbed. A chorus of crickets filled the air. Night was nearing. The sun touched the peaks to the west, and a golden light bled across the mountains. The end of the day was here. It was almost time.

At last he reached the path he had come for. A knife ridge extended before him, a game trail following its crest. Jeremiah hiked along, picking his way carefully among the stones and grass. To either side the ground dropped away, falling thousands of feet into canyons below.

The sharp edge he had been hiking on blunted, widening out into a small field atop the peak. This was it. Stunted high country trees stood scattered about, their branches swaying gently in the evening air. He walked slowly through the grass toward the far edge.

"This is the place I will kill myself," he whispered.

He had found it many years ago. He had been hunting a wolf that had been killing calves on the ranch. He had tracked it for two days and was going to kill it, conservation laws be damned. It had led him here, along the ridgeline to this little field, and then stopped. As Jeremiah had come up the ridge, rifle in hand, he had seen the wolf. It in turn had seen Jeremiah coming and sat out in the open, unable to flee with the cliffs on all sides.

It was small for a wolf, but there was no mistaking it for a dog or a coyote. Its fur was jet black, and like all wolves, it had paws as big as a man's hands. Two bright yellow eyes stared at Jeremiah as he approached. It was cornered, and they both knew it.

Jeremiah had raised his rifle and aimed. The wolf had faced him, meeting his gaze with its own. There was no fear in its eyes. It breathed calmly, deliberately, completely in control. Neither moved. Something Jeremiah could not explain passed between them. He had taken his finger off the trigger, lowering the rifle.

The wolf had sat a moment more and then stood and walked right past Jeremiah. Once it was gone, he had walked out to the edge of the field where the wolf had faced him and looked down. He was thousands of feet above Three Rivers, able to see the horizon in every direction.

That was a long time ago—after his father's death, but before his son's.

Before now.

———

Jeremiah stopped at the edge of the field, where the sky met the grass and the ground dropped away.

This was it.

The end of the trail.

He took off his jacket and sat down on a large stone, looking out into the canyons below. Distant peaks cut into the darkening sky of the horizon. The first star appeared overhead. The churning of Three Rivers began far below, its roar echoing up through the peaks toward the sky.

Jeremiah looked down at his hands, opening and closing them. As he opened them, he remembered the first time he had ever held Jonathan, so small and warm and pink.

Images poured forth from his palms. Again and again his son's face rose. First a tiny newborn, then a kicking baby, wiggling arms and legs in the air, and then a two-year-old chasing their lab, Colt, through the house. Jeremiah sat transfixed, watching the boy rise out of his palms and grow. Jeremiah smiled, and Jonathan smiled back—that crooked, goofy smile that always lit up his face when he saw his dad.

The images began to blur and fade. The boy disappeared, replaced with an image of the holster, spinning slowly in its eddy.

Jeremiah's heart hardened. He brought out the bullet. He held it up between his index finger and thumb, slowly rolling it back and forth, back and forth. The little lines and grooves in the metal jacket reflected the setting sun. Jeremiah stood the bullet upright in the palm of his left hand so that its tip pointed toward the sky.

He stared.

The same hands that moments before had offered him his son's face now offered him a bullet. He placed his palms together, hands touching as if in prayer, and then transferred the bullet to his right hand.

He drew out his father's revolver, feeling its weight, hearing the slight sound it made as it scraped against the holster. He popped open the chamber and inserted the single bullet, one step from the firing pin. He snapped it shut, its loud click audible above the chorus of crickets. He felt faint. With a surge of anger, he jammed the gun back into the holster.

Three Rivers, so far below, roared louder.

Jeremiah lay back against the stone. He looked up as the first stars pierced the fading light. He felt the cool of the rock against his back. He smelled the dry pine and the dust of August. He tasted the salt of his sweat on his lips. He felt his chest pound with the contractions of his heart.

He closed his eyes.

The holster still spun.

He opened them. Shaking now, he steadied his breathing. The fingers of his hand slid down over the rough handle of the pistol, now cool to the touch. He would stop the holster spinning once and for all.

The world around him began to warp and weave into meaningless patterns and colors and sounds. Only the revolver was clear, loaded with its lone bullet. He took a deep breath, placed it against his right temple, and paused.

Son, here I am.

He took his last breath and squeezed the trigger.

Nothing happened.

He squeezed it harder.

Again, nothing.

Desperation overcame him. He put the gun in his mouth, grabbed the trigger with both hands, and squeezed as hard as he could. Still the trigger would not move, would not budge. Shaking so hard he nearly dropped the gun, he took the revolver out of his mouth.

He brought it slowly down into his lap. Waves of nausea and adrenaline washed over him. He looked at the pistol, seeing but not comprehending.

There, sticking out of one of the bullet chambers, was a foot.

He still didn't understand. He brought it up to his face in the fading light. There, in one of the six chambers for bullets, was a tiny red plastic leg with a lightning bolt on it, jamming the pistol. The hammer was pulled back, but the cylinder couldn't advance with the leg jammed into it.

He stared for a full minute and then looked down at the holster on his waist.

A small plastic figure lay in the bottom of the holster with one of its legs broken off. The remaining leg was caught in a hole in the seam of the leather at the bottom of the holster, trapping it in place. It was the action figure Jonathan called The Bolt, his favorite. He must have left it there after playing with it for the last time.

It dawned on Jeremiah, slowly at first and then with a force that threatened to tear him to pieces—his son's last act in life had been to place his favorite plastic toy in a spot where it would hold death back from his father. A small piece of plastic shaped like a leg had stopped Jeremiah from killing himself.

The impossible had occurred.

The son had protected the father.

Something broke inside Jeremiah, and he began to sob. Grief ripped through him. It overcame his very being with the force of three rivers colliding in a flash flood. He screamed into the night sky until he was hoarse, his cries ringing out into the vastness. The mountains accepted his grief. They stood solid and still in the face of his suffering, as they always had. As they always would.

He cried at the beauty. He cried at the horror. He cried at the beauty and the horror that all of life is. He cried until he was empty. He collapsed back, exhausted, staring at the stars. They pulsed overhead to the rhythm of the mountains, the rhythm of the rivers, the rhythm of Jeremiah.

He closed his eyes.

It was gone.

The spinning holster was gone.

He lay empty for a moment, just being with the silence. Some broken part of him had been put back together just enough that he knew he could go on. He could still be.

And then he remembered. His wife and daughter. They were still in this world.

He was still in this world.

He stood up slowly, straightening his back, brushing the dust from his pants and clothes. The crickets had stopped. The three rivers below were quiet. It was night now. He spoke out loud to himself.

"I'm only a night's hike away from the truck." He paused. "I can be home by dawn."

"*Home*." He said it again, carefully emphasizing the word, speaking it out loud to feel it on his lips, to make sure it was real.

He picked up his father's gun. In the moonlight, he could still see the small foot jamming the hammer open. Grabbing the little foot with his right hand, he twisted it back and forth, easing it out of the revolver. He popped open the chamber and took out the bullet.

In one hand, he held the little leg; in the other, he held the bullet. He paused, understanding now what he held in each hand. He drew back his arm and threw the bullet over the ridge, as hard as he could. It twinkled briefly in the sky and was gone.

He carefully put the little plastic leg back into the holster. He unfastened it and set it down next to him. He knew what to do.

Stone by stone, he built a rock cairn at the cliff's edge. When he was done, he reached into the holster and gently freed the tiny one-legged figure, The Bolt, from where he lay stuck in the bottom weave of old leather.

Jeremiah hung the holster over the rock cairn so it faced the cliff's edge, in the direction of the coming sunrise. And then, very carefully, he placed The Bolt just inside, his little plastic arms over the top lip so that he could see the mountains. Just as Jonathan would have wanted.

He turned to go and then stopped, seeing the gun.

There was one more thing.

Stone by stone, he built a second, slightly larger, rock cairn next to the first. When he was done, he lay the revolver at its base. Just like his father would have wanted.

He stood for a moment between the cairns, a hand resting gently on each, looking out at the mountains.

An elk bugled in the night. Somewhere, far away in the canyons below, another called back.

Jeremiah shouldered his pack.

It was time to go home.

———

For some, grief is an illness, an infection. But for others, a lucky few, it is a dust. And if you can survive that initial storm, when the sky turns black and dirt falls in great clumps from the sky, if you can do that and just hang on, you will discover something.

The dust left behind by grief is really soil, richer and deeper than any you can find on this earth. Collect it, gather it gently together inside of you, and wait.

In the same way a great tree must first take seed and then be given space to grow, the memory of those you have lost seeks a place to put down roots. Give grief time, and in turn, it will give you what you seek—a place for the memory of your loved one to reside inside you for the rest of your days.

That is the purpose of grief.

Drowning

A twenty-eight-year-old woman drowned next to me in a hot spring. I didn't know it at the time. While she inhaled liter after liter of 130-degree water barely more than arm's length from me, I was at peace, floating on my back and staring at the stars like a blissed-out astronaut tumbling through the Milky Way.

When people drown, whether in a two-inch puddle or in the depths of the Pacific Ocean, it is the lack of oxygen that kills them. All it takes is three minutes—180 seconds. I am sure this is not news to you. More than once, I have stood in the trauma bay and asked myself how bodies strong enough to survive metastatic cancer, flesh-eating bacteria, or even massive traumas can be snuffed out with nothing more than a cupful of water. Even submerged tissue paper lasts longer than we do.

And yet, when the woman next to me drowned and I missed it, I was left shaken. Suddenly, I was not so sure of my role in this world. I had not been ready. Not by a long shot. And it got me thinking.

A decade before, a medical student rotating through the department had asked, "If there is one skill that defines emergency medicine, what is it?" At the time, I could not answer. I spouted some standard lines about constant readiness, managing airways, and identifying sick or not sick—all basic ER skills. But it left me unsatisfied. Some part of me knew there was a more truthful answer. Something about emergency medicine that was uniquely ours. Something *we* were the experts at.

But whatever it was, I couldn't place it. Cardiologists knew more about hearts, orthopedists knew more about bones, neurologists more about brains. For every case I could think of in the ER, it seemed there was always a specialist with a greater level of expertise and knowledge than our own. And no matter how many cases we saw, it didn't matter. We could never approach their level of expertise because we were expected to know something about everything instead of everything about something.

Were we just the garbage men and women of medicine, there to pick up the scraps, to fill the space between arriving at the hospital and going upstairs to see the real doctor? I wasn't so sure anymore.

I tried out different definitions. For a while, I would have told you emergency medicine was defined by its taking care of all comers, no matter how trivial or catastrophic their complaints. Emergency medicine was really just a sum, a total made up by adding together seven thousand sore throats, a billion dental pains at three in the morning, and the fifty drug seekers who show up every year on the Fourth of July, trying to con you into a handful of Hydros.

But over time, I grew dissatisfied with that definition as well. There was more to the ER than just its parts, just like we are more than arms and legs and organs.

Then I thought that maybe emergency medicine was defined by the shift work. The nights and days and swings that shuffle constantly. Little by little, they slowly wear you down like pennies dropped in your pocket. A few hundred is no big deal, but fifteen years in, you start to feel it in your joints. Those pennies start to feel an awful lot like bricks.

And then other times, I would have told you that emergency medicine was about the saves, no matter how you got them. About the shotgun blast to the belly that kept bleeding out no matter what you tried. About the surgeon calling on her cell phone to say she had had a flat tire and had to hitchhike to the hospital. About how, finally, you just stuck your fist in the hole and leaned on the bleeder with all your weight. Your hand cramped, and your back spasmed. But somehow it worked. Ten minutes later, a beat-up van skidded to a stop out front and the surgeon ran into the ER, red faced and breathless. And the patient survived.

Or maybe I would have told you it was defined by the other kind of saves. The homeless alcoholic you sent to rehab fourteen times in a row, who—on the fourteenth time—discovered sobriety, transforming from a gutter-dwelling mess into a radiant jewel of a human being. A jewel that lit up the entire town. You were part of that. And now, when he or she helps other alcoholics restart their lives, a tiny piece of each victory is yours. It's like a pyramid scheme of goodness that never stops giving.

And yet, I realized that none of these were what made emergency medicine what it is. Yes, they were pieces that added together to build the specialty of ER, but you could remove any one of them and the specialty would still stand. They were like Jenga blocks, for lack of a better analogy. But the piece I was after was the cornerstone. The one that, if removed, would cause the whole tower to crash down in a noisy mess. That piece, whatever it was, was *our* specialty.

And until that night in the hot spring in the mountains of Idaho, it was completely invisible to me.

It was the end of a week-long motorcycle trip with an old friend of mine from high school. We were riding dirt bikes, Yamahas, with camping gear strapped to the back. It was, and is, an annual tradition each fall. It's a week I look forward to all year long. A chance to just be. To ride dirt bikes and talk about motorcycles and mountains instead of bronchiolitis and bowel obstructions.

It was the last night of the trip. I was beat. Buzzing along on a dirt bike at forty-four years old no longer feels quite like it did at seventeen. But what makes the swollen joints and aching back worth it is the chance to stumble on places that stick with you for a long time. And that night, the night the woman drowned, we stumbled on a place that will stick with me forever.

It was late in the day, and we were searching for a spot to camp. A few random turns from one dirt road onto another, and to our delight, we stumbled upon a ten-foot circle of stones below the road. Inside the stones was a pool of water, crystal clear and steaming.

A hot spring.

The pool was wedged between the bottom of a steep, sandy bluff and a river. Scalding water bubbled up and out of the side of the bluff, superheated somewhere in the earth far below. It drained down the hillside in little streams that steamed and bubbled and smelled of sulfur. Instead of flowing directly into the river below, the streams were captured by the circle of stones, forming a waist-deep pool.

On the other side of the pool, the riverside, several brick-sized rocks could be added to or removed from the wall. If you wanted to heat the pool, you simply blocked the inflow of the river, allowing the bluff water to collect around you. To cool it, you pulled up the rocks blocking the river water, and cold water swirled into the pool, dropping the temperature.

Usually our motorcycle trips took us so far into the middle of nowhere that we ended up camping on our own—no one else was around. But to our surprise, there was already a couple at the hot spring, a man and a woman who appeared to be in their early thirties. They floated in the pool as we pulled up, their sunburned faces relaxed and smiling. The man gave us a wave and invited us to join them.

Two hours later, as the sun set, the four of us soaked in the pool, steam billowing up the canyon walls around us. We chatted about favorite camping spots, hidden trails, and the best back roads that weren't on the map. But eventually the conversation grew quiet. The stars came out. The heat and steam transported each of us off into our own worlds.

An hour passed.

Two hours passed.

By then, the night air was in the low thirties. The hot water in the pool steamed continuously, blocking out what little light there was from the stars. Soon, holding my arm directly out in front of me, I could not see a thing except the darkness. I was effectively blind.

And then, sometime around one in the morning, it happened.

I remember the moments before. I had been resting the back of my head on one of the stones. It fit my neck and skull perfectly, cradling my spine like one of those inflatable pillows you see people sleep with on planes. It allowed my body to float effortlessly, encapsulated by the water, by the valley, by the night.

I had such a deep sense of peace, of safety, of being right where I was supposed to be.

Even as I write this, I still have a hard time comprehending that at those very moments, two feet away, a woman was drowning. At some point, she quietly lost consciousness and slipped beneath the water, her head swallowed with the rest of her by the pool. If I had known, I could have reached out and saved her.

But I didn't.

That moment disturbs me. I pride myself on being aware of the world around me. Of always watching, always waiting, always being ready. When I see a toddler playing on a riverbank, some part of my brain runs through what I'm going to do if she falls in. When I sedate a patient for a procedure, I set out all the airway equipment I could possibly need should things go south. If he quits breathing, I will be two steps ahead and breathing for him with the gear before the first missed breath.

When I was a resident, I had an attending physician who used to quiz me. "What is this person going to need in ten minutes? Best-case scenario? Worst-case scenario?" He would ask me where the necessary tools were and why I didn't have them in the room already. He forced me to practice a ten-minutes-in-the-future kind of medicine so that whatever happened, I was ready.

It has served my patients well, and it has become so ingrained into me that it is almost a religion—a faith in worst-case scenarios. But instead of the second coming of Jesus, I'm waiting for that sudden complication: the child here for ear pain who suddenly chokes on a hot dog in the waiting room or the staff member who suddenly blacks out next to me at the computer station.

I am always ready. Always ten minutes ahead.

So perhaps that's why it bothered me so much that I was floating in that hot spring adrift in the present. I was not ten minutes ahead. I was not running through scenarios. I just was.

There was probably a moment when she realized she was in trouble. That it was up to those around her to do something. But the call of the dark was too strong, like that moment on a long road trip when you are falling asleep in the back seat of a car with your neck all weird.

You know you should move it or you are going to wake up sore, but you are a breath away from sleep. The quiet hum of the road, the warmth of the heater, the *swish-swish-swish* of the windshield wipers in the rain—it's just too overpowering. You fight for a second to move your neck, to sit up and readjust, but then it's just too much and you let go, slipping into sleep and the night. That is what I imagine death is like.

In retrospect, I think she lost consciousness from sitting too long in the hot water.

When she lost muscle tone, her body simply collapsed beneath her, her head sliding into the water and disappearing like the last little bit of a sinking ship going under.

For a while, I even thought our greatest expertise in emergency medicine was our *lack* of knowledge, our ability to practice medicine in a place I call the Gray Zone. It's a place that is exceedingly difficult for most of the obsessive-compulsive types who go into medicine.

In the ER, sometimes we have to be able to discharge a patient home without knowing exactly what is wrong with them. We just have to know they do not have a life-threatening condition. It's not satisfying, for us or the patient, but sometimes it is all we can offer. To say, "I don't know, but it's not dangerous." And to be right.

We often have to act without prior medical history—not allergies, not medications, not even a name. When a car rolls up and dumps out a naked, gray, and unconscious nineteen-year-old woman before speeding away, you aren't allowed the luxury of taking a thorough past medical history. Your job is to save her.

The second piece of not knowing means there are times when you have to make a choice. Send home someone who you think is sick but can't figure out why, or swallow your pride and ask for help.

The last chip you can play for your patients is the dreaded phone call to a specialist—the nephrologist, the cardiologist, the gastroenterologist. "I don't know exactly what's wrong with my patient. His blood work is normal, and his tests are fine. But there is something that worries me about him. Something bad. And I need you to come evaluate him."

Those are some of the hardest words for a doctor to say. As you can imagine, those words often elicit an eye roll—or worse—and a lecture from an annoyed specialist, especially at three in the morning. Those moments are hard; I am not going to lie. But you are there for the patients, not for yourself.

A friend of mine once told me that the hardest part of being a surgeon is knowing when to stop cutting. I would say the hardest part of being an ER doctor is knowing when to stop trying and just ask for help.

The alternative is the doctor who refuses to admit that he doesn't know what's going on. The doctor who can't acknowledge that he or she is wrong. The doctor who tries to force the patient to match the incorrect diagnosis instead of just stepping back and getting a fresh set of eyes to help out.

First, do no harm, Hippocrates said.

Second, ask for help when you need it.

But sometimes you are in a place or time where you cannot ask for help. Like a hot spring in the mountains.

For some reason, around one thirty in the morning, the woman's husband flipped on his head lamp. None of us had spoken for at least an hour.

The light went on, and the beam cut across the pool, only to find her spot empty. It took a second for our brains to process what we were looking at. Because there she was, under the water—pasty gray, eyes wide open, hair floating around her face like a sea anemone in the changing tides. Right next to me. At arm's length.

The three of us dragged her out onto the rocks. I remember the smell of sulfur, of hot springs, the freezing air, and the fog billowing and flowing around us. It was like we were trapped in a cloud. Five steps in any direction, and you would disappear.

Her husband had the only light. A head lamp. I remember that beam. It seemed so solid, so defined as it gyrated back and forth and up and down through the fog with his screams. It was so crisp that it looked like you could reach out and grasp it with your hand and tear it from the air. As he scrambled over the rocks, the beam bounced around, lighting her face off and on like some sort of short-circuiting spotlight at a mountain rave. I finally grabbed it from him and shone it in her face. Two giant black pupils stared back at me, oblivious to the light. Not a good sign.

I remember that.

I remember thinking, *Oh no, oh no*. But there was nothing to do. We couldn't call for help; the nearest phone was sixteen miles down a potholed one-lane dirt road and then maybe another hour on the highway to a town of two hundred people. And even if we could have called them, then what?

She was dead now.

I remember how heavy her body was as we dragged it out of the springs. It was hot, too hot, from being too deep for too long in the

130-degree water. I remember how her head flopped down as we dragged her from the pool and set her on the rocks.

I remember the river roaring.

I remember her husband screaming, and I remember my friend yelling her name over and over. I remember the light beam in the fog dancing like it had lost its mind with the rest of us.

We all panicked.

And then it happened.

I remembered that this was my job.

That this was *me*.

And suddenly I wasn't afraid.

I knelt on the rocks next to her and felt for a pulse. It was there. Faint, so fast I couldn't count it, but there. I pulled her jaw forward, my index and middle fingers just behind the angle of her mandible—the jaw thrust, it is called. I did it exactly as I had done more times than I can count on old ladies, middle-aged men, blood-covered teens, even premature newborns who would fit in the palm of your hand.

I pulled her jaw forward, clearing her airway, and water poured out. I remember it landed on the rocks next to her face and steamed and twisted skyward like some mystical poison spilling out of her.

I waited.

And then, to my surprise, came a gasp. A raspy, choking, brain-stem-mediated, gurgling gasp.

But a gasp.

She vomited water from the hot spring, gallon after gallon it seemed, dumped from her lungs and stomach to steam on the rocks at my bare feet.

I no longer heard her husband's screams or the river roaring. I no longer felt the icy air. I was no longer aware of anything other than this woman—my patient.

I hit her on the back with an open hand, a slap really. The painful stimuli caused another gasp, like a baby's first breath after being spanked on the butt. She coughed and gurgled again. More water came out.

I leaned down close to her. I knew what to say. "Take a breath if you want to live." And to my delight, she did. She took another breath and retched.

I counted the seconds in my head before the next breath.

Forty passed. Not good.

I slapped her back again, the smack of skin like a whip cracking in the night. "Take another breath, or you're going to die."

She did.

Her husband, understanding now, leaned close and shouted, "Don't leave me! Take a breath; take a breath; take a breath!"

And she did.

Resuscitating her was like reeling in a ten-ton blue whale hooked on the end of a spider's thread. One wrong move, and the thread would snap as she dove for the depths, gone from this world forever.

But she didn't leave. The thread held. And we nursed her back.

Breath.

By breath.

By breath.

And then I remember how cold it was. We were all soaking wet in the fog, in the middle of the night, and she was still flopped on her side on the rocks.

I remember a new fear set in. That she had been submerged too long. That I had not done her—or her husband—any favors by bringing her back. That she was just an empty shell that would live another fifty years in a long-term care facility. That she would have a trach to breathe through, a peg tub in her stomach for tube feedings, an adult diaper, and bedsores over her back and buttocks from days spent unmoving in bed.

One summer in high school, I had worked in a nursing home. I knew what her room would look like; I could imagine the faded photos of the beautiful young woman she had once been, maybe a stuffed animal she had loved as a child placed next to her by long-gone parents. Other than that, the room would be bare and sterile. The TV would play from dawn to dusk, and she would never move, never look at the screen, never do anything but breathe, shit, and stare at the wall. I knew exactly what might await her, because I took care of those people all the time in the ER.

All because someone had dragged her from a hot spring in the mountains and saved her.

But it turns out I never have any idea what is going to happen next. Maybe that's the very best part of being alive: the surprises you don't see coming.

We dragged her up the bluff, still completely unconscious. We dropped her twice, flat on her face. She was still wet, and if you have ever carried an unconscious person up a loose and gravelly bluff in your bare feet in the pitch black, you know how hard it is.

I remember her head kept flopping back and staring at the sky. We stopped and pushed it forward and flipped it down, staring at her feet.

But we did it.

We got her to her husband's van, dried her off, lay her on her side, and squatted on the floor of the van together, the three of us strangers no more, waiting to see what would happen.

An hour passed.

She continued to breathe, her breath now regular.

At some point, the coughing began.

She coughed and coughed and coughed.

And then the most beautiful, impossible thing I have ever seen happened. Her candle relit. Her flame flickered back to life and cast light upon the world once again. Her pupils constricted. She blinked, she swallowed, she moved her arms and legs, and she frowned and looked at us, her face filled with fear.

"What just happened?" she asked in a hoarse voice.

I smile when I type that; it's exactly what I am still wondering.

She recovered completely, 100 percent. I can't explain it. She was submerged in hot water. The worst kind. Her lungs had been filled with steaming spring water that smelled of sulfur. And yet there she was, blinking and coughing and holding her husband's hand. She was a save. The best kind.

A few weeks later, her husband tracked us down on Facebook. It was surreal, to say the least, seeing pictures of her with her husband, with her parents, with her friends and family. Still alive and going through life. Her presence lighting up the world.

Maybe it was fate, and she would have survived whether or not we had randomly taken that road to the hot springs. But maybe, just maybe, she survived because I was there. Because I knew what to do. Because I could stay present and think. Because I had stood in the fire for so long at work that when the world around me lit up in the middle of nowhere, the heat couldn't touch me. My scars turned out to be my strength.

And as the sun rose and I sat in camp the next morning, wide-eyed and disbelieving, it hit me.

I had been asking the wrong question.

When you strip away every single part of what we do, I mean really strip it all away, down to the very core of what it is, you arrive at this:

Emergency medicine is to be present when no one else can be present.

When a mass shooting occurs, and ten ambulances show up at the door, your job is to be present. Calm, thoughtful, active, but most of all, present.

When you step into a patient's room and your mind is boiling from the colleague who just chewed you out, or the administrator who second-guessed you, or even the drunk who took a swing at you, when you step into a new patient's room, push that all away and be present.

When a child dies and there is nothing you want more to do than to run away from the grieving mother and lose yourself in the next patient or chart, stay. Stay and be present for the mother. Don't hide from what you are there for.

And take pride that you are a specialist.

A specialist at being present for moments that are too hard for anyone else.

Synesthesia

A patient was shot and killed with his own gun in the middle of an emergency department where I once worked. We later learned that the patient had come to kill us. When we cut off his clothes with the trauma shears to code him, we found black metal clips of nine-millimeter ammunition taped to the front of his chest and belly, the shiny metal sticking out like necrotic tumors from some awful cancer growing deep inside.

He was carrying enough bullets for all of us—he must have planned to spread that cancer to every doctor, nurse, tech, and clerical worker in our emergency department.

By accident, by design, or maybe by both, a high-school wrestling coach visiting a sick friend collided with the man as he stormed out the door of his patient room—arm extended before him and gun drawn, ready to kill. The coach wrestled the man to the ground, a gunshot was fired, and the patient died, right there on the linoleum at the foot of the nurse's station.

Part of the ER closed for an hour while what seemed like the city's entire police force descended on the hospital. But there was nothing to do. The man was dead. So they took some pictures and statements, interviewed witnesses, and went back out on duty. The man's body was draped in a sheet and wheeled to the morgue downstairs, with all the others. Housekeeping mopped up the blood and wiped down the wall of the nursing station with antiseptic. Half an hour later, everything looked the same as it always had. The ER was fully open for business. Drunks wandered in, people on crutches limped out, and the waiting room filled right back up. Everything went back to normal.

But I didn't feel normal. Someone I had never met had wanted to kill me. A slightly different roll of the dice, and these pages would still be blank. For the first time in my career, it struck me in a visceral way that I could no more stay untouched by the constant trauma around me than I could stay dry standing outside in a downpour.

The realization frightened me, and it got me thinking.

You can catch just about everything by working in an emergency room. Tuberculosis from the coughing patient who lies about his travel history. HIV from that unlucky needle stick while suturing. Even plain old influenza from the little kid who sneezes on you as you listen to her chest. Name an infectious disease, and you can probably find a health-care worker who contracted it from caring for a patient.

It's just part of the job.

But what if the disease was the suffering itself and the risk factor for infection was proximity? I had spent a lot of time around suffering, maybe too much time. If there was something to catch, more likely than not, I already had it.

A crazy thought hit me. What if the world as I knew it was not at all how the world really was? What if this odd disease, this emergency-medicine disease, had somehow already changed my perception of reality without my ever realizing it?

Several years ago, I took care of a local jazz musician who taught music at the high school. His name was Abel Finley, and his was one of those bizarre cases that you encounter in emergency medicine maybe once a decade. I saw him for a rare type of stroke that had left him with a condition called synesthesia. People experience synesthesia when stimulation of one neural pathway fires off another unrelated pathway. In other words, it's as if someone wired together unrelated things in your house—you open the cupboard over the sink, and suddenly the sprinklers in the yard go on. It doesn't make sense.

Unfortunately for Abel, he had the worst kind of synesthesia a musician could possibly have. With his rare stroke, he lost the ability to hear music. He could still hear the sounds individually, but the melody—the music part of music—was destroyed. Synesthesia had crossed his neurons with his sense of taste.

Now, the flavor of a hot dog might cause him to hear the sound of a church bell, or he might experience the flavor of an orange as the noise of a jackhammer breaking apart cement. Meanwhile, the sound of a trumpet playing Louis Armstrong's "Swingin' at the Savoy" suddenly sounded like nothing more than noise. It sounds crazy, but it's a real thing.

I visited Abel on the rehab floor a couple of times after he left the ER. To say he was not doing well would be an understatement. The world he had known for sixty years had been ripped out from beneath him by the stroke, leaving him in a foreign place devoid of the thing he loved most.

Remembering him, I suddenly knew what my disease looked like. Unlike Abel's condition, which had overcome him in a matter of minutes when a tiny clot blocked a vessel and a cluster of neurons died, mine had come on gradually: I had emergency medicine synesthesia. My own distorted perception arose not from a clot, but from repeated exposure to trauma. And instead of transforming flavors into sounds, my synesthesia caused the good things in the world to appear bad.

If I witnessed a miraculous recovery from cancer, some part of me saw it as only a temporary success. My synesthesia focused my brain on the fact that in the end the patient would still die. If I sat in the bleachers at a football game, all I saw were terrible possibilities just waiting to devastate the people around me. The obese man huffing and puffing up the stairs? He was a heart attack waiting to happen. Those kids playing at the top of the bleachers? They were a foot away from an inevitable fall and a grievous head injury. You name it; wherever I looked in the world, I saw only the possibility for bad outcomes. My wires were as twisted as the branches of a thorn bush.

No wonder I was depressed.

A decade and a half in the ER had changed me into a glass-half-empty kind of guy. Some would say I was just another jaded ER doc, burned out on humanity. But now I knew the truth: I had a disease. A sickness.

I had ER synesthesia.

I read once that when a Native American looked at a tree, he didn't see a tree at all—he saw wood for a fire, branches for a roof, bark for a canoe, and tree limbs for a bow. When I looked at a tree, I just saw a tree. But God forbid I look at a poorly lit two-lane highway with a blind curve.

The worst part was that I had no idea what to do about it. I didn't want to quit my job. I couldn't quit my job. But I didn't want to stay sick, either. I had to find a way back to health.

So I began to study my disease. Instead of lab tests and animal studies, I had only the history of myself. Somewhere along the way, I had wandered off the path of hope and become lost. I thought back to the beginning.

————

When you are new to emergency medicine, it is the trauma that attracts you. How can it not? It burns so bright and seems so new that everything else in the world grows bland by comparison. *This*, you think to yourself, *this is what I've been searching for.* The first time you see a chest cracked open and a dead person brought back to life, it sends a jolt down your spine all the way to the soles of your feet.

The early years of ER training are like standing at ground zero as nuclear fission occurs, only it's not radiation that's released—it's stories. Stories that are told and retold, sometimes just until the end of the shift, but sometimes for decades: the man who partially decapitated himself with the homemade propane tank on Christmas Eve. The four-year-old boy whose right arm was torn completely off at the elbow by the family pit bull. The unbelted expectant mother ejected at sixty-eight miles per hour from her Honda Accord and found standing on the side of the road in the rain, not a scratch on her body.

When you are young, you want to be there for these things, no matter how awful they are. Any emergency-medicine physician or ER nurse who tells you otherwise is lying. You want to stand as close as you can to death and destruction without experiencing your own.

I heard it said once that the reason our legs grow weak when we stand on a cliff's edge is not so much the fear that we will fall off, but the fear that we will throw ourselves over. And standing in a trauma room when things go south is as close as you can get to the rocks below without being on the gurney yourself.

Of course you want to help people, to make a difference, to make the world a better place. But there is always another reason, an unspoken reason, that doesn't make it onto the medical school application.

The years pass. You work hard. Little by little, the suffering around you starts to add up. You don't notice it, but the seeds of synesthesia cling to you. It doesn't matter if it's a screaming one-year-old with an earache or the death of half a family in a house fire. Suffering is suffering.

The seeds take root and begin to grow. You can't feel them. You are young and new to the ER. You have work to do, waiting rooms to clear. You chug your half gallon of coffee or your two liters of Mountain Dew on the drive into work. You crank some heavy metal on the radio and push on full steam ahead. You arrive and power through the work, swept away by the bright lights of the trauma bay and the blood splattered on your shoes by the end of the shift.

But you start to feel weird. You start to have strange thoughts. One day on your way to work, you see an eighteen-wheeler coming at you on the two-lane highway and think, *If that driver had a seizure at just the right moment, I'd be like that patient I coded last night.*

And there's not a thing you can do about it.

You push the thought away, but it returns. And others follow. So you begin to compensate. To find ways to tame the things you have seen and the things you have heard, even if you are not aware of it. You look to your colleagues across the specialty, and you see how they deal with it when no one is looking: divorce, alcohol and drug abuse, gambling, suicide, health problems, high-risk self-destructive behaviors...

Oh shit, you think.

They live in the world of emergency-medicine synesthesia. Shadows have crept so slowly over everything that they failed to notice that their world has gone dark. Their souls harden. Callouses develop where before there were none. And it doesn't stop. The next shift brings another rape victim, another dead child, and another drunk found in the ditch, all in a row. You find yourself with no emotional response at all. You are empty.

You can see where I am going with this.

When that shooter died in the ER, it was like a slap in the face to me. I had already been struggling, but his death pushed me right over the edge. Or maybe it woke me up. Either way, I didn't like it.

There was only one thing to do. Put myself under the microscope. Try and catch the disease as it spread; try and see how it worked. Maybe then I could find a cure.

Physician, heal thyself, I said to myself.

All I needed was a case.

I didn't have to wait long.

———

We take care of inmates from the state penitentiary in the emergency department where I work. I often wonder if some of the older ones struggle with the same issues we do. If perhaps when they were young, they were called by a different kind of siren. Only instead of a trauma room, it was the charismatic kid next door dealing crack cocaine under the streetlight. Too interesting to stay away. Too exciting to ignore. One thing led to another, and now it's eighteen and life to go.

I can always tell when a prisoner from the penitentiary has arrived in the department. You hear them before you see them. There is a jingle of chains and a shuffle of feet as if Santa, fresh from rounding the world on Christmas Eve, is staggering down the hall in an exhausted stupor.

The inmates wear orange jumpsuits made of a stiff, rough cotton, a number in black ink stamped on the front left breast. Instead of a zipper up the front, the suits close with a narrow strip of black Velcro. The jumpsuits' legs and sleeves stop just above the ankles and wrists to make room for cuffs.

Inmates enter the ER festooned in chains. A long chain encircles the waist and locks in the front, just below the belly, like a belt with a padlock instead of a buckle. Through the top of the padlock feeds a vertical chain. It, in turn, locks on to a horizontal handcuffs chain, which also runs through the top of the padlock. Ankle cuffs connect their feet, and they in turn connect to the bottom of the vertical chain.

The end effect is that if inmates try to lift their hands above their waist, it pulls up on their ankles and vice versa, limiting their ability to strike, kick, or run. The chains become like the block and tackle used in a shipyard, only there are hands and feet pulling against each other instead of boxes and lines.

The inmates always come with an entourage. If they are near the end of their prison sentence and are staying in the lower security wing, they are accompanied by just two uniformed guards. Often, in the fall, as I step in and out of the room reporting lab tests and x-ray results, the two guards and the prisoner will be watching the *Seahawks* on the TV above the door.

If Russel Wilson is playing well, there will be laughter and clapping. If he throws an interception, booing and jeering. On those days, I've often thought the only things missing are a couple of empty boxes of Domino's pizza and maybe a few six packs of Bud Light. The inmates seem like any other patient—save for the fact they are handcuffed to the bed.

At first it bothered me. They were prisoners, after all, and felons at that. But over time, as I saw more and more prisoners, I learned that many of them are no different from you or me, except perhaps for the misfortune of being in the wrong place at the wrong time.

Imagine being eighteen and sitting in your car on a hot August night—window down, engine running, listening to music and waiting for your best friend to hurry up and grab a pack of smokes. The new girl said she would be at the party down by the river, and she hoped to see you there. You are thinking about the way she looked at you when for no reason you will ever understand, your buddy decides to gun down the 7-Eleven clerk for the twenty-six dollars and eighteen cents in the register.

And you are now the driver.

These types of prisoners, the bad luck ones, are usually the politest of all my patients. "Yes, sir." They nod when I tell them to stay off that foot until the swelling is gone. They never argue or talk back or threaten the staff. They thank us at the end of the visit. When they are done, they stand up and shuffle out the ER doors back to the white transport van with the bars on the windows, chains jingling and guards on either side.

Of course, they aren't all like that. It's a penitentiary, not a jail. There are prisoners there who make your skin crawl, who drop the temperature of the room with their very presence. Even though they are cuffed to the bed in two places, and four guards armed with assault rifles stand at the bedside for the entire visit, your mouth grows dry and your palms sweat when you talk to them.

Interacting with those patients is like looking into a black hole. No light escapes. And even though it's dark, you can sense something moving down in the depths of those prisoners, something *other*, something that sees you as an object to be consumed.

But at least you can see their fur and fangs and feel their bloodlust as you put your stethoscope on their chests. It's clear what they are from the start. You quickly learn to be mindful of your hands and arms, keeping them where they can't be suddenly grabbed or bitten.

I used to Google prisoners after I met them. As we talked, I would try to deduce their crimes by our interaction alone. Could I learn to read them the way I had learned to spot a case of appendicitis in the way a patient walked? With a little practice, I got pretty good at it. It turns out a lot of murderers actually look and talk like murderers.

But then there are others who defy all categorization—a man I'll call Kip, for example. I remember him well. He was a year older than I was—forty-five, according to the chart. But if you walked past him in the gym, you would have guessed midthirties, maybe even late twenties. It was the way he moved. From the slightest flex of his fingers to the easy nod of his head, every motion had a smooth, crisp quality. It was like his joints were filled with WD-40 instead of synovial fluid. It made you want to stare. It was like watching an elite dancer or martial arts master practice his craft. There was just something about him.

I don't know how, but Kip was tan. He had that rare type of skin that seems to incorporate its own protective coating: immune to sunburn in Fiji, immune to pallor in a prison cell. He was sitting on the edge of the gurney when I came in, casually reading a beat-up copy of *Principia Mathematica*, the chain between his wrists hanging down like a stainless-steel bracelet. He was relaxed, and his ankles were crossed. He could have been a grad student sitting on a park bench on a summer day, lost in a textbook as geese lazily circled on a pond before him.

When I stepped into the room, he stopped reading, pausing for a moment to lean forward while he brought his chained right hand up to his mouth. He licked his index finger and creased down the top corner of the page he was reading to mark his place. He folded the book gently closed.

"Hey, Doc." He smiled as if we were old friends and in a liquid motion tossed *Principia Mathematica* to one of the guards. The guard caught it with one hand and set it in his lap. It struck me as a funny gesture for a prisoner, as if the guard was his assistant or employee.

Kip shuffled a step toward me and extended his right hand, only to have it yanked short by the chain. He smiled sheepishly and shrugged. Normally, prisoners are not allowed to stand without a guard in arm's reach. But not Kip. Out of the corner of my eye, I noted that the guards were now ignoring us. One of them was showing the other vacation pictures on his phone. I see the guards all the time as they bring down various prisoners. I trust them. They were not concerned, so neither was I.

I stepped forward and shook Kip's hand. It was a manicured hand with no callouses, trimmed nails, and a healthy firm grip. He looked me in the eye as we shook and nodded with an easy confidence that established us as equals. His actions were those of a man of power—someone who had been the CEO of a large corporation or perhaps the longtime chief of surgery at a major hospital.

The population up at the penitentiary changes all the time. More than one CEO has rotated through up there, some for embezzling millions, some for vehicular manslaughter, and some for plain old murder after catching a wayward spouse with the pool boy.

Kip sat back down on the gurney, and I sat down on the stool next to the bed and got to work. He'd been having headaches for the last couple of weeks, pain bad enough that they were waking him up at night. Last night's was the worst.

"I've never been sick a day in my life," he told me. He twisted the chains in his hands as he spoke, the way a bored girl absent-mindedly twists curls in her hair. "I have enough to deal with right now without this."

I ran through a review of symptoms. He denied them all. No blood in stools, no fevers, no weight loss, no cough, no chest pain, no weakness in an arm or a leg, on and on.

"No, no, and no," he said, sitting back in bed and folding his hands in his lap to hide the chains.

"Any other major changes?" I asked.

"My new home isn't quite as nice as my old one." He smiled, and the guards laughed on cue at a joke they had clearly heard before.

Kip's face grew serious. "It's been a stressful adjustment for me, to say the least."

I spent a few more minutes talking with him. There was something marvelous, almost magical about him. I'm sure you have come across one or two people like Kip. They are the ones that cameras panning the crowd at sporting events always end up on—not because of their looks, but because they glow in a way that makes them stand out in a crowd. They shine like a lighthouse, irresistible to the other people around them.

Both male and female nurses who glanced in as they passed the room came back a minute later to see if he needed a blanket, or a cup of water, or anything else. He even hit it off with the registration clerk when he rolled in with the computer, somehow figuring out in about two seconds that they were both University of Washington alumni. He connected to every single person who walked into that room with mind-blowing ease. As someone who interacts with people all day, it was a joy to watch. He was a master.

Kip smiled and joked and worked the crowd like Bill Clinton in his heyday. He was quick and witty, with a funny story for just about everything.

When I told him that I was going to order a CT scan for his head, he nodded approvingly, and part of me felt pleased that he approved. By the time I left to go put in the orders, his room was like a party.

Moving on to the next patient, a ninety-two-year-old man with dementia, curled on his side in a diaper, felt like stepping into a house with the curtains drawn after spending a day at the beach out in the sun.

When I got back to the doctor's station, I had to know.

I couldn't resist. I was almost positive I remembered reading about a Tech CFO up at the prison who had been sentenced for embezzling almost twenty million dollars. It had to be him. If I remembered correctly, they'd never found the millions. I smiled to myself, imagining Kip getting out of prison in the near future and sitting on a beach somewhere with his hidden millions, one step ahead of everybody.

I sat back down at the doctor's station, tilted the monitor so that no one could see what I was doing, and Googled his name.

His picture came up right away.

But he wasn't a CEO.

And he wasn't a chief of surgery.

He had been a janitor at a grade school on the other side of the state, and he'd been arrested at a routine traffic stop for expired tags. In the trunk of his car was a dead six-year-old girl.

That arrest led to several other charges of kidnapping and murder.

I closed my eyes and sat back, sick to my stomach.

There was no doubt it was Kip. The mug-shot photo matched the man in room eight to a T. He was even grinning in his arrest photo, eyes twinkling with delight as if it was all a joke and he was the chief prankster.

But it wasn't.

If you've ever wondered what emergency-medicine synesthesia feels like when it first infects you, there it is. It's that moment when reality breaks apart in your hands like a dried-up clump of dirt in the summer. When what you thought was solid turns out to be nothing at all. When the wires cross in your head and rewire themselves all wrong.

I leaned back in my chair and looked down the hall. Kip was sitting on the edge of his bed again, a nursing student and a medical student standing in front of him, giggling like schoolgirls as he told another story. He saw me staring and waved. I waved back, not knowing what else to do.

It turned out that Kip had a brain tumor. A huge brain tumor. He'd been having headaches because it had invaded a blood vessel, which was starting to bleed into his brain. I admitted him to the hospital. That night, it let loose, hemorrhaging like a broken water main into his skull. Kip died at three fourteen in the morning, lying on the operating table with his head cut open.

When I came in to work the next day and found out that he was dead, I didn't know what to feel. Part of me said it was a good thing—good that the world was rid of a monster and good for his surviving victims and the families of victims long gone. Maybe his death would give them just a sliver of peace. The more I thought about it, the more I was glad that he had died. To this day, I'm still not sure what that says about me. It feels weird to rejoice at someone's death, at anyone's death, no matter who they are.

But part of me did.

Over the years, I have taken care of the victims of people like Kip. They are not abstract ideas to me. For your sake, I will spare you the details.

I stopped Googling prisoners after that.

The day Kip died, I had parent-teacher conferences for my children after work. I was standing in the hall with my wife and kids, waiting for our turn with the teacher, when the janitor came by.

"Hey, Greens," he said.

"Hey, Davy!" all three of my kids said at once.

He smiled and high-fived each of them as he passed.

For a moment, I thought I was going to be sick. I watched him mop his way down the hall, just some random janitor, my stomach churning. My logical brain knew that Kip was the exception to the rule when it came to janitors in grade schools, but some other part of me was screaming.

And then I knew this was it. This was the disease. There could be no clearer example.

For the next several months, I struggled. Now that I was aware of my sickness, I saw that it had infiltrated every part of my life. I could hear it in how I spoke to my kids about playing too close to the street. If I woke in the night, I could feel it making me look out the window for prowlers. Even driving down the street, I could feel myself bracing for a crash. It was a miserable way to live.

Four months later, the universe finally tossed me a lifeline.

I was sitting at the nurse's station, trying to recover from an awful morning. I had been taking care of a girl with intractable seizures until the helicopter had taken her away. I was finishing her chart when it happened. A name popped up on the computer: *Abel Finley*. I stared at it for a moment, trying to understand just why it sounded so familiar. And then I remembered. It was Abel, the man with the stroke.

I clicked on his name and signed up to see him, barely able to contain myself. It had been six years since I had seen him in the ER, and I was filled with an overwhelming curiosity. What had happened to him? The last time I had seen him he had seemed on the verge of suicide, overwhelmed by what he called "the noise in my head."

I read through his records, just to be sure it was him. There were no visits for the last six years. I skimmed his chart notes from his time in rehab after the stroke. The very last one stuck out. "Patient is not doing well, seems to be struggling with sensory overload but further therapy not indicated as benefit lacking. Discharged home to follow up with primary-care physician."

I went in and introduced myself. He had sprained his ankle and just needed an x-ray. The ER was slow, and he seemed in no hurry, so I sat down and told him I was there on that day when he'd come in six years ago with the stroke.

"So what's happened since?" I asked.

I expected him to talk about depression, about what he had lost that day, about the struggles he had gone through trying to adjust to his new world. I thought at best maybe he would have eventually given up and accepted what had happened to him. Maybe he could tell me how to accept what had happened to me.

Instead, he laughed and said I wouldn't believe it if he told me.

"Try me," I said.

He shrugged. "I'm a chef now." His eyes twinkled, and it was clear he was about to tell a story he loved to tell. "We're just back in town visiting some old friends. I own a restaurant in Seattle now."

That was a surprise. I crossed my legs and interlaced my fingers, leaning back against the counter.

"I never cooked a day in my life before the stroke," Abel said. "But that first night home, I sat in the kitchen as my wife made dinner. She had some butter sizzling on the stove and threw in some garlic. The smell made my head explode with sounds. The synesthesia."

He paused, frowning at the memory.

"It was awful. Just noise. Just like it had been in the hospital. But then the strangest thing happened. I kept listening to it. I had a crazy music teacher once who insisted that if you listened long enough, you could find music in anything. So that's what I did. I just sat there and fought the urge to cover my ears."

I sat forward on the stool, trying to imagine what it would be like to hear sounds with every smell and taste.

Abel continued, "The sounds were awful. Like an ice pick in my skull. So bad that I got up and threw an onion in the dish, and then—boom!" He threw out his hands, mimicking an explosion, and his face lit up with a smile. "The most beautiful sound filled my head."

He closed his eyes and pretended to be a conductor, waving an invisible baton to a beat only he could hear. "I picked out some more spices, smelling each one and listening. I matched the tones and tossed them in. And suddenly it was a symphony in my head instead of just noise."

He opened his eyes and laughed, the delight in his voice filling the room.

"My wife said it was the best meal she had ever tasted. After that I started cooking, using the sounds to guide me. I kind of got obsessed with it, and I started to cook all the time. I forgot all about the trumpet, about my life in jazz, about my stroke. I cooked for everybody: first for my wife and then for friends. And suddenly, people wanted my food. I couldn't taste it, but I could hear it. My stroke gave me a chance to see the world in a new way, but it was up to me to figure out what to do with it."

I sat there for so long with my head spinning that he finally coughed awkwardly. "Now, about my ankle, Doc?"

The x-rays were fine. Just a sprain. I splinted him up and sent him on his way. I wished him luck with his new life. But I knew he would be OK. He had figured out his synesthesia.

That night I got home late. I grabbed a beer and sat at the kitchen table, the house quiet. Everyone was asleep. I thought about Abel. About his music teacher who had said there was music in everything if you listened closely enough. I thought about the man who was shot in the ER and about Kip. I thought about all my patients. I thought about everything.

I tried to listen to all the stories in my head. They were jammed together, all playing at the same time like a fifth-grade band class trying to play a tune.

I stared at the table in front me, my mind drifting. One of my kids had left out a notebook full of homework. I tore off a page of lined paper and picked up a pen. I stared at the blankness before me and let the noise get louder in my head. I didn't fight it. I just tried to listen.

I closed my eyes, thinking about an upsetting case I had had a day ago of a girl with seizures. The image of her seizing kept replaying over and over in my head.

And then, to my astonishment, I heard something. Three words spilled out of me.

"Break seizure break."

I wrote the words.

A second sentence followed.

And a third.

I wrote a short story about a patient, a girl with seizures. It barely filled two pages. It was sad and terrible, but in it there was a quiet music about life and loss that I could just hear.

For some reason, I felt a little better. I put the pen down and went to bed.

My wife woke me in the morning, the story in her hand. She had been crying.

She hugged me.

She loved the story.

So I wrote her another one.

And the more I wrote, the more I began to hear the music. Some part of me began to rewire itself.

My wife shared the short story I wrote with a friend, who shared it with another friend. They liked it.

So I wrote another one.

And then I wrote a book.

"Keep writing," people said. But I wasn't writing. I was listening. Listening to the synesthesia in my head as it lit up the world around me, chasing away all the shadows with colors so bright and beautiful that I could hardly stand it.

I found I had something to say about emergency medicine, about life, and about death.

So I did.

About the author

Philip Allen Green, MD, is board certified in emergency medicine. He works full time as an emergency medicine physician in Walla Walla, Washington. His previous book, *Trauma Room Two*, has been praised for its originality and authenticity in revealing the life of an ER physician. When he is not working in the ER he can be found spending time with his family or exploring the Blue Mountains of eastern Oregon.

69052214R00100

Made in the USA
San Bernardino, CA
10 February 2018